SEVEN GROOMSMEN FROM HELL

A REVERSE HAREM ROMANCE (LOVE BY NUMBERS BOOK 6)

NICOLE CASEY

CONTENTS

He was awful to me in high school, but now he and his six friends want me?

The moment I saw him, all I could think about was the way he used to torture me.

6 foot 2, sky blue eyes, dark buzzcut hair; that's what my personal demon looked like.

He was my greatest fear, and when I had nightmares, he was the star.

10 years later, and now when he slips into my dreams, he brings six other men along.

They look at me with lust in their eyes and a glint of hope for something more.

Seven circles of hell; each of these men wore one like a fresh pressed suit and tie.

They're interfering with my job and with my life.

I've always been resilient, but every woman has her limit.

How can I do my job, when all I want to do is them?

I wiped the wisps of sweat glued hair out of my face, and packed my water bottle and towel into my gym bag. I'd just finished another of 'Lady Kate's Killer Pilates' sessions and was near to collapsing. Dinner and a shower, and I'd be lucky to make it to the bed before passing out.

"Okay," I said to Anna, who was the demon who convinced me to join her in the sessions, "what's the big news?"

Anna, a cute, tall and slender woman with black hair in a pixie cut and dark blue eyes, reached into her bag for a moment before whipping around brandishing a black, velvet box. She tipped the lid aside revealing a stunning, pink-gold, diamond ring. By my estimate, it was twenty grand at least, but Kent was a world-renowned football player, so it was probably chump change for him.

"He did it! He proposed!" she yelped.

I let out a little screech. I wasn't a chipper, cheer-for-everything kind of girl, but Anna had been head over heels for Kent for a while, and I was excited he finally popped the question.

"Congratulations!" I grinned from ear to ear as Anna pulled the ring from the box and slid it on her finger. I raised an eyebrow. "So… who's the wedding planner? I happen to know someone?"

Anna put the box back in her gym bag and pulled the strap over her shoulder. "Oh, I went with someone from my job who does it on the side." I frowned and then Anna let out a huge, barking laugh. "I'm *joking*. Obviously, I want you to plan my wedding, you dope. And none of this 'family discount' nonsense either. It's your business and I support you, so I'm paying full price."

The notion made me fuzzy inside. "Thanks. When can I get started?"

"I was hoping you'd ask that." Anna reached back into her bag and when she came back that time, she had a huge, dark blue binder. "Here are a few things to get you started."

I took the binder, feeling its intense weight threaten to make me drop it. "A few?"

Anna laughed. "Well, I've been planning for this day pretty much ever since Kent asked me on our first date."

I flipped open the lid to the binder and looked at the front page titled, 'NECESSARIES.'

One Bride (Me)
One Groom (Kent)
One Bridesmaid
Seven Groomsmen
Destination:Puerto Rico
Date: Christmas Day

"Destination wedding, huh?" I said, "And who's the one bridesmaid?"

Anna smiled at me. "Who else, but you?" she said sweetly. "That is, if you accept? Will you be my maid-of-honor?"

I couldn't believe it. I knew Anna was without siblings, but I never thought I was who she would want to hold such a prestigious title on her special day. "Of course!" I threw my arms around her in a huge hug, nearly killing us both with the binder. I pulled away and tucked it in my gym bag as we headed for the door of the studio. "So, who are the groomsmen?"

Anna's mouth curved down into one of strained 'uh oh.' "So, here's the thing. Despite my begging, Kent has insisted on bringing his seven best friends as his groomsmen. Five of them he plays football with, his accountant, and a doctor he knows from his head injury."

"So, what's wrong with that?" I asked.

"They're a *bit* of a handful. Let me be more specific, they're a handful when they're on their *best* behavior, when they're at their worst..." Anna's voice trailed off like she didn't want to say more for fear of scaring me off.

"They're men. Throw 'em some beers and a porn magazine and you have them eating out of the palm of your hand," I joked.

Anna shook her head. "Not these men."

"What's so wrong with them?" I said.

Anna tilted her head in thought for a moment as we walked down the street in the brisk, Texas air. "So, you know all those rumors that Christian Bale freaked out on some extras on set and is secretly a huge jerk in real life?"

"Yeah?" I said.

"And how Ken Jeong seems like a dufus, but he's actually a doctor and super smart?" she continued, and I nodded. "And how drop dead gorgeous Jason Mamoa is?"

I imagined Aquaman's bulging muscles and tribal tattoos. "Oh, he really is."

"That," Anna said. "That's what's wrong with them."

"Which part?" I asked.

"All of it," Anna responded.

I shook my head with a chuckle. No man was truly like that. "I'm not worried about it. You just worried about getting married. I'll handle the men."

1

KHLOE

could still clearly remember the moment it all went wrong; the day Anna asked me to be her wedding planner. That memory faded from my mind like a bad dream. It was now just a week and a half until the wedding, and in that time I'd learned that these seven men were even worse than she described.

"Lord, give me strength," I said aloud to myself as I stood at the entrance to a popular restaurant in downtown Austin.

Inside the restaurant were eight men, only one of whom didn't make me feel like jumping head first into a wood chipper. Kent was the fiancé of my best friend, Anna, and he wasn't a terrible guy, though I could certainly judge him for the company he kept. The other seven men inside the restaurant were his groomsmen. Seven loud, annoying, yet undeniably sexy assholes with a penchant for making me consider becoming a serial killer. There was something about them; they were each like fingernails on a chalkboard in their own, annoying way, but they also could have me hot and bothered inside of five minutes. It was infuriating. Why did seven such beautiful men on the outside have to be horrendous brutes on the inside?

I took a deep breath as I looked myself over in the reflection of the restaurant windows. I thought I looked okay. I was a thicker girl, with full thighs, a pert peach ass, and a DD rack. In my youth I considered myself 'chubby,' daresay even 'the fat girl,' but as I got older, I learned that men preferred having a little more meat on the bones. I worked hard to keep my stomach relatively toned, but made no attempts to be some skinny mini like a magazine barbie doll. I was full figured, and I liked it. Still, the groomsmen—the best man in particular—knew how to press my buttons, and my size was the biggest one. So I wore a long sleeve t-shirt, jean capri pants with design-intended rips, and had my brown hair falling in waves on either side of my face, to mask some of the chub to my cheeks.

I pushed open the door and made my way in, already preparing myself for the worst. They were all staring back at me, waiting to pounce the second they saw me.

There was David Jackson; all the guys called him 'Doc.' From what I'd gathered in the time I'd spent with them, there was no basis for the nickname, they called him it just to mess with him. That said, he was the health conscious one of the group, and had a physical education degree to boot. He was a tall, solid-build running back with dark, short cut hair, caramel skin, dark brown eyes, and a clean canvas; no facial hair, no tatts. He was as good-looking as they came for a blemish-free guy. I preferred the rugged look, but I certainly wouldn't kick Doc outta bed. Well, I would, but it wouldn't be because of his looks, it would be because of his near-incessant tendency to try and convert everyone around him to veganism, complete with judgmental looks at every bit of an egg or burger.

Next to him was Brett Townsend. Dark choco-late skin was a perfect frame for his dimpled smile, short beard, and light hazel eyes. His hair fell in short, wild dreads across his head, ticking the poorly retouched tattoo of a former lover's name scrawled across his neck. Of the groomsmen, he was probably the friendliest, but he was as stubborn as a mule. He refused to be one-upped, which meant if all the guys were participating in making my life miserable, he was falling in line if not trying to top the troop.

Christian Hill was the linebacker of the same team Brett and David played for, the Hellraisers. He was a thrill seeker who took great joy in anything that made his heart beat a little faster. He had tan skin, bright green eyes, feathery, dirty blond hair and a smile that could kill. He was incredibly tall, and liked to use that height to tower over me and make me feel small, though I couldn't keep myself from imagining myself all over his massive size.

Mason Lee was called "Old Man", though he was only a year or two older than the rest of them. His nickname was given to him more because of his appearance than his age, and because he'd already been married and divorced once. He was tall too, but was a stockier build and had sea blue eyes that were hypnotic if stared into for too long. He was a 'friendly chat you up until you can't escape' kind of guy, with ruddy cheeks and undeniable charm. He was 'dad' until he was 'daddy.'

Dr. Cody Williams was not a football player like Kent and the others, but was actually a doctor. I didn't actually have any idea why one of Kent's groomsmen was a doctor as opposed to more of his football buddies. In the beginning when I was trying a 'kill 'em with kindness' approach to relating to the men, I tried to ask, but Dr. Cody had a terrible habit of making me feel like an idiot. I stopped trying to speak with him after the third time he used pandering sarcasm to explain something to me. Unfortunately for me, he was one of the best looking of the group, standing at just under 6 feet, with a lithe but muscular body. He had a square face and green eyes with short, dark russet hair, and almond skin. He was a stone cold stunner. If he hadn't gone for medical school, he could have been a model, not that I would ever tell him that.

Of the guys, Bram Russel was my favorite, in the least of all evils kind of way. He wasn't a complete ass, and was smart, so he didn't often get sucked into the ribbing and teasing most of the guys hit me with. That said, he was impatient and didn't often stick around for antics. I couldn't count the number of times I looked up needing Bram for one thing or another and he'd just left. He had cocoa skin, a little bit of height too him, and boasted impressive muscles for an accountant. With his dark gray eyes, near buzz-cut black hair, and fresh, tattoo free skin, he had a mysterious, bad boy kind of look.

Last, but certainly not least, Luke fucking Heath. The resident ass-in-chief. If the groomsmen were an army of jerks, Luke was their idiot general. He was Kent's best friend and was the quarterback of the football team aka the star and he wanted everyone to know it. I went to high school with him and he was just as much of a punk back then. He had made it his personal mission to make my every waking second a hell on earth, finding creative, annoying ways to destroy everything he touched. Sure, he was sexy, if you could get past the incessant irritation. He was tall, had naturally tan skin, crystal blue eyes, and the biceps of a guy on the cover of a romance novel. He had dark hair in a buzz cut and a barely there goatee, and had a tribal tattoo sleeve covering his left arm. If I could expel any of these men from the earth, he'd be the one. I could navigate Mason's manipulative conversations, Dr.

Cody's 'I'm smarter than you' snobbery, or David's 'holier than thou' health shtick, but if I never had to see Luke again, it would be too soon.

I stared at them all, trying to convince myself that I'd made it this far, it made no sense to go back now. "'I'll handle the men,'" I mocked myself. "Boy was I wrong."

2

LUKE

$\mathcal{I}$ was surrounded by my closest friends at a steakhouse restaurant in downtown Austin, but their absent chatters could not be further from my mind. I had my eyes trained on the doorway. On the other side, forming a tantalizing silhouette through the frosted glass, was Kent and Anna's wedding planner, Khloe. That's who she was currently, but I'd known her since high school. I could say that back then wasn't different from now. I still loved to tease her the second she arrived anywhere around me, but unlike back then, when I did it now, it was because I couldn't control how attracted to her I was. She'd been their wedding planner for months, and with just weeks to go until the wedding, I could damn near say I could take the world record for longest, unsatiated hard-on.

The door opened, Khloe finally walked in, and I didn't even wait a second to respond. I cupped my hands on either side of my mouth and shouted, "Shut up, guys, our personal slave driver is here."

"Really dude?" Kent said, with genuine irritation in his voice. "Slave driver? She's planning my wedding."

"Is 'slave driver' the best you can do?" Khloe barked, her eyes narrowed at me with contempt. "And here I actually thought I had to be worried today."

My eyes lowered as well, but mine were animalistic, and hungry. The only person around for miles who didn't know I wanted Khloe, was the woman herself. Maybe she was just blind to the obvious, maybe it was the fact that I was hiding my attraction behind playful teasing, but either way, all of the other groomsmen and even Kent were in the know. The groom-to-be had already threatened me on more than one occasion to completely dismember me if I didn't keep my hands to myself. I promised him I would be good, but I may have had my fingers crossed behind my back when I did.

I leaned towards her. "Would you prefer 'Madame Sade' instead?"

"Luke," Kent hissed a warning. "Be nice. Quit giving her shit. You already ran her through the ringer trying on every suit but yours at the fitting last week."

I grinned remembering myself trying to squeeze myself into Brett's too small suit. I purposely did so outside of the dressing room to flash my package towards Khloe as best I could. She had to be at the fitting because all of the arrangements were in her name, and I was hellbent on making that process as much of a headache for her as I could.

"What do you want from me?" I retorted. "They all looked like the same monkey suit to me."

"Well after next week, you'll never have to wear that monkey suit again," Kent snipped back.

"I'll be blissed to burn that piece of trash suit the second I step out of it," I said, then I turned and looked at Khloe. "And don't act like you didn't love watching me get undressed. I saw you checking out my junk. If you wanted a closer look, all you had to do was ask."

I leaned in even closer, but bringing my face any closer to Khloe was probably a huge mistake. Her sweet, flowery perfume wafted into my nose and coaxed me towards her like a bewitching finger steaming off of a cartoon pie. It was apparent in the slight pout to Khloe's lips and puff of her cheeks, that she believed I was just living up to my inner-asshole by messing with her whenever I got the chance, when really what I was doing was likened to seasoning a dish before eating it. I wanted her, probably more than I'd ever wanted anything. I wanted to slam her on a bed and strip her clothes off until those beautiful curves were completely exposed to me. I wanted to see her lips parted just so, moaning as I drove my dick into her until I was cumming all over those huge, full breasts.

All of that would have to wait though. I was running the risk of being ex-communicated and possibly murdered if I touched her before the wedding.

A week and a half never seemed so long.

3

CHRISTIAN

"Yes, I was looking," Khloe admitted in response to Luke, shocking us all, "but I was only trying to verify that you weren't, in fact, a woman, given how little there was to look at. What that Tanner bitch kept bragging about back in high school, I'll never know."

"Oh!" All the groomsmen erupted into playful jabs at Luke's expense.

I chuckled at the mention of Luke and Khloe's history. Khloe, of course, thought Luke was just being the same high school bully he'd always been, but we all knew that Luke had it bad for Khloe. He had ever since she first signed on as the wedding planner. He seemed content to let her think it was the former, so we did as well.

"That was cold," David said with a laugh.

"That was deserved," Kent added quickly. "Maybe he'll learn to keep his mouth closed." He picked up his steak knife and pointed it in Luke's direction. "And if you dare burn the suit from my wedding, I'll lift the 'you can't kill my groomsmen ban' on Khloe *and* Anna. See how you fare then."

"Oh, please do," Khloe said. "I've got a running list of all the ways I'd like to do him in."

"It's a farce anyway," I added, balling up one of my napkins and tossing it at Luke's head. "Luke's such a cheapskate, we're going to be seeing that suit at every marginally formal event from now until his wedding, hell, maybe even his funeral."

"What's the difference?" David replied, taking a healthy chug of his beer. "Wedding, funeral, tomato, to-mah-to." He held his mug up towards Kent in a 'cheers' type motion. "Rest in peace, brother."

Brett reached across the table and swatted David across the back of his head. "Maybe the reason we call you 'Doc' is because you need a psychiatrist."

Kent clapped his hands. "Guys, focus," he said. It took everyone a bit of time to calm down, but eventually silence befell the table and Kent motioned over to Khloe. "You have the floor."

Khloe smiled and it instantly piqued my interest. She was attractive, there was no doubt about that. When we weren't giving her shit, her face had this calm, inviting look that made me want to sit down and get to know her better.

"Well, I won't take up much of your precious time," she chided, the smile fading from her face. She reached into the red purse hanging over her shoulder, with the bag situated at her waist, and brandished a set of white envelopes. She started to hand them to each of us, all with our names written on the front. "Thanks to Kent's big bucks, the travel arrangements to Puerto Rico have all been made, for my sanity, without your help. We'll be staying at the El Conquistador Resort, and you all have all-inclusive, round-trip ferry rides to the Palomino Island where the wedding is. Your time is mostly your own, all I ask is that you're punctual for the rehearsal and punctual for the wedding. Be brutes on your own time please."

Luke tossed his hand to his forehead like a soldier to a captain. "Yes ma'am, loud and clear. Anything else."

"Why yes," Khloe said with a faux-sweetness, leaning in towards Luke. The tension between them crackled through the air. "If any of you miss the plane and end up costing this couple any more money than they've already spent, I will blind you with a spoon like they did that boy in Slumdog Millionaire."

Luke's jaw tensed. He wanted to pounce. "You won't touch me."

Khloe tilted her head, not realizing just how badly she was taunting the beast. "You'll never see me coming."

She stood up straight to address the group again with a clap of her hands. "I know that we haven't been a match made in heaven, but it's not about us, it's about Kent and Anna. So please get home safely, get to the wedding, and then you'll be free to go your way, and I'll be free to stop giving a damn."

She didn't wait for a response. She turned, flicking her hair about her full face, and left.

The guys all remained quiet as she walked out. It was unspoken among all of us, Kent included to a certain extent: Khloe was fucking hot.

Kent finally let out a hollow whistle and tapped Luke's shoulder. "Wanna get the next round with me?"

"I would," Luke responded, grabbing the bottle nearest him to empty it, only to discover it was already empty, "but my dick is harder than a fucking post. Rain check?"

He too didn't wait for a response. He stood up from the table, and stormed from the restaurant.

Kent sighed. "What are the actual chances he's able to resist her until after the wedding?"

I shook my head with a chuckle. "Why don't I buy *you* the next round?"

The rest of the guys started laughing because we all knew that those chances were probably zero.

4

KHLOE

I felt like one of those cartoon characters with steam coming out of their ears. If all I had to do was usher six of those assholes through this wedding, I could probably do it without issue, but throw Luke into the mix and it made me want to give Anna her money back and walk away without another word. Every person who offered me a friendly smile and a "Happy Holidays!" as I walked along ran the risk of getting full-fledged cussed out as I wanted to take my anger out on anyone or anything I could.

It was a good thing when I was finally angrily shoving my apartment key into the lock to let myself in. "Fucking asshole Luke," I hissed. I stormed into my apartment, tossed my purse and keys to the table by the door, and made my way immediately into the kitchen for a bottle of wine. "Wouldn't touch him? He'd be dead before he heard me." I popped the cork and, not even bothering with a glass, I pressed the glass bottle to my lips and tipped it, tasting the sweet, white wine as it passed down my throat.

I spent the next few minutes changing into more comfortable clothes. I donned a pair of leggings and one of my favorite fuzzy hoodies, put my hair up in a messy bun and then returned to the kitchen to make a mimosa and pretend I wasn't just flat out day-drinking. I went and curled up on my bed, played music, and did my best to calm my mind, but it didn't work. As I was sitting there stewing over Luke, my mind drifted back to my high school days. I was the resident fat-girl, and the target victim of the head cheerleader Tanner and her boyfriend Luke. My weight was just a gateway drug to 'ugly,' 'nerd,' and 'idiot,' despite the fact that I have always been quite beautiful, never considered myself much of a nerd, and always got above average grades.

I assumed they just liked picking at the low-hanging fruit. One time, I was coming back from gym class and went in to change, to find that my clothes were gone and only a three sizes too small cheerleading outfit was left in its wake. With no way to call for help, and no one around but undoubtedly the bullies who were torturing me, I had no choice but to squeeze myself into the cheer-leading outfit to at least go for help. When I opened the door to leave, at least half the cheerleading squad and their football boyfriends were standing there, cameras ready, which immediately started flashing the second I appeared. The blinding bright flashes paralyzed me in fear until I was finally able to back up enough to re-enter the locker room, slamming the door shut behind me.

I wasn't certain how long I holed up in that locker room, crying my eyes out until they were raw, but eventually a guidance counselor came, who brought me a pair of sweatpants and a t-shirt, and helped me get out of the locker room and home without additional ridicule. I couldn't go to school for an entire week after that, and when I finally did return, I found that my tormentors' punishment was so light that they were still giggling and pointing at me when I returned. A mere slap on the wrist for a lifetime of emotional damage.

That was what I had for memories of Luke, and when I saw the other groomsmen with him, they reminded me of those assholes snapping pictures of me back then. He was as big of a jerk as they came, and any company he kept had to be just as bad; of that much I was certain.

I wasn't sure exactly when I had fallen asleep, but I was awakened from my sleep suddenly by the sound of knocks on my door. I checked my watch and noticed it was almost midnight. Who the hell would be at my door so late? I rushed to my door, and opened it, shocked to find that my friend Jordan was standing on the other side. Her blond hair was a mess across her head and her red eyes were swollen and red.

"Jordan?" Jordan was an old friend of mine that lived in Dallas. "You look awful." I hugged her, pulling her inside and shutting the door behind her. "Well, you don't look awful. You look beautiful as always, but you look like you've been through hell."

"I have been," she replied. "Can I stay with you for a few days?"

I couldn't imagine what she had been through to make her suddenly need to stay with me, but if it was that important, it was worth refuge. "Of course. What's going on?" I set her bags aside, helped her down to the couch, and then skipped to the kitchen to make her a mimosa and grab her a bowl of ice cream. I returned and handed them to her. "A mimosa." I settled down onto the couch next to her and then tapped her leg. "Okay, out with it."

I listened as Jordan explained the situation she was in with the six men she'd fallen in love with back in Dallas. She started out as the nanny for their single dad's club and eventually entered into a relationship with all of them. Unfortunately, she'd just received a random tip that one of them had killed their ex-wife, and she was worried she might be next. She was still trying to figure out what to do and needed to stay with me for a few days.

Looking for a distraction, I decided to exchange stories with her about the seven idiotic groomsmen that had been forced upon me. I regurgitated to her in fierce detail the different bad manners of the seven jackasses I was tasked with corralling, spending probably too much time venting about Luke.

"You did say when I spoke to you back at the beginning that you thought they were going to be a handful," Jordan said.

"I was right three months ago; feels the same now." I looked at Jordan and she looked exhausted. She barely touched her ice cream or mimosa. I tapped her leg. "Come on. I have a spare bedroom with a super comfy bed you can stay in."

I got Jordan comfortable in the spare bedroom and watched as she immediately passed out, but with a forlorn expression on her face. I felt glad that I wasn't in *that* situation. At least I hated the men I was intertwined with for the moment. I cleaned up our dishes and then returned to my own room and then drifted off back to sleep.

5

MASON

Grocery shopping was my least favorite adult activity. At one point I considered paying someone to do it for me, but they didn't get any of the things that I liked. After trial running a delivery service, I finally just decided to do it myself. In most cases, I considered it a nuisance, but god must have decided to award me for committing to such a mundane task because as I was sifting through the ribs, who else should round the corner, but Miss Wedding Planner herself. She looked more tantalizing than any of the meats in the section. She was wearing an army green, form-fitting romper, and a pair of roman sandals. Her hair was up in a ponytail and she was amusingly concentrated on the big cuts of beef.

"Are you hoping it'll talk to you if you stare at it long enough?" I asked.

Khloe looked over, and then as soon as her eyes

landed on me, she rolled her eyes. "Hey, Old Man." She looked back at the meat. "I'm going to a party and I need big pieces of meat." I snickered at the phrasing and then burst out laughing. A woman like her saying something like that was too good for words. She glared at me through a half-lidded gaze. "What's so funny?"

"You really should be careful what you say in public," I responded. "Lest you get the wrong kind of 'big meat.'"

"You have a dirty mind," she growled back. "I expected more from you. Maybe something immature like that from that moron Luke, but you're the mature one of the group, or so I thought."

She didn't wait for a response from me. She decided to abandon her meat and started to walk around me. I wasn't the kind of guy that appreciated a woman walking away from him, or anyone for that matter, so I decided to say something that I thought would catch her interest.

"You know less about Luke than you think," I said.

"I know exactly who he is," Khloe retorted as she passed.

"You don't know that he wants to bend you over," I spat out.

There was a rattle to Khloe's cart as she tripped over her own feet. The wheels screeched as she whipped it back around and turned to face me again.

"What?" she yelped. "You're even crazier than I thought, Old Man."

I snickered at the look of bewilderment on her face. I had her; hook, line, and sinker. "I'm crazy, but not about that."

"How do you know that?" Khloe asked.

I shrugged. "I thought you had some meat to get to."

Khloe pointed a finger at me. "I control your life for the next two weeks. You *will* tell me."

I clenched my jaw. Khloe just didn't realize how much of a tease she was. Telling *me* what I will and won't do? I would love to show her exactly who was in charge between the two of us. There was more than one reason why that wasn't a possibility, so I would at least settle for watching her squirm a bit more.

"I'll tell you," I said. "Meet me at my car outside after you're done with your shopping. I'll answer any questions you have."

"You sound like a creep offering candy," Khloe responded.

I grinned. "Then I guess we'll just have to wait and see if you come to the unmarked white van."

That time it was me who didn't wait for a response. I pushed my cart away from her, smiling wide at the feeling of her eyes on me as I walked away. I finished grabbing my last few items, checked out, and brought them out to my red Dodge Charger. I leaned against the hood and took in the slightly cooler Texas air as I waited to see her leave the store. I knew she would come, but I anticipated she would stall a little bit; did she really want to know the truth about Luke?

Eventually, I saw her rolling her cart out of the store with a purpose. She was storming right towards me and, damn, that girl was too sexy for her own good. The shorts of the romper clung to her thighs until the fabric gave way to her smooth, milky skin, and her breasts were spilling out over the top of the v-neck of the top. I could see myself flat out ripping it off of her and replacing it later; she was a temptation on legs.

When she finally made it to my car, she jabbed a finger into my chest. "Out with it."

I motioned my head back towards my car. "Get in."

"Get in?!" she barked. "Next you're going to ask me for my social security number."

"Come on, stop being so dramatic. You want to know, don't you? He's a famous football player, I'm not gonna talk about him out in the open," I explained.

Khloe looked around the parking lot of the grocery store and then finally rolled her eyes and walked around to the passenger side of the car. She climbed in, and for a brief moment I did imagine driving off immediately, taking her to my house, and having my way with her, but I abstained. The smell of a flowery lotion filled my car and reminded me how much I missed the general presence of a woman around me. I could only imagine the rest of the guys felt the same, most of all Luke. There was just something about having access to something sweet that Khloe was giving me intense desire to have.

"Okay, I played your weird grocery store secret game, I'm sitting in your car. Tell me about Luke," Khloe demanded.

I laughed. "There isn't much to tell. He's got the hots for you. Bad."

Khloe scoffed. "That's a lie."

"Believe me. I've seen enough of him nearly busting out of his pants to tell you with certainty. The man wants you bad. We all know it, even Kent, probably Anna too. The only one who doesn't know it is you," I explained.

I'd heard through the grapevine that Khloe and Luke had history, and not the good kind. He was a high school bully, and she was his victim. Hearing that he was attracted to her now had to be a bit odd.

"You're positive?" Khloe asked.

"I'm not a liar," I responded. "But listen, he would skin me alive if he knew that I told you. So because I told you, you have to promise to continue to play dumb."

"Believe me, I will hardly have to play at it," Khloe responded.

I decided to keep to myself that I was attracted to her too. I probably could have revealed some further information that would benefit me more, but it seemed more fun to just piss Luke off instead.

"This will be our little secret?" I said, holding my finger up to my lips.

Khloe sighed, still looking dumbstruck. "The secret is safe with me."

6

CODY

It had been a long week at the hospital, so I was glad when Kent invited me out to lunch and, thank god, the A&E department was slow enough that I was actually able to take a break to go and meet him. After doing a final check-in with all of my current patients and checking in with the nurses, I packed up my things and left the hospital. Kent sent me a text that he wanted to meet at a small bistro that was one of our favorites. The rest of our friend group ate almost exclusively at restaurants where the women wore short shorts and cleavage-revealing shirts, so when we wanted to satiate our more refined palettes, we had to do it alone.

The sun was shining in the sky and it was a relatively warm day, so I decided to walk instead of drive. I hadn't spent much time outdoors lately despite being an avid runner. I mostly had to settle for taking a few laps around the employee gym at work, so I was excited for the opportunity to get out and enjoy some fresh air.

Kent was a good friend. I wouldn't know any of the other guys in our group if it weren't for him, and really, I probably would be a lonely, workaholic loser with no friends.

ߎ

"Dr. Williams, we have a concussion coming in. A football player that took a helmet-to-helmet." The announcement from the trauma nurse in passing sent shivers down my spine.

I was new to the field, and new to the hospital, and I'd specifically been avoiding brain trauma. Those were one of those areas where patients tended to die on the table, and I was still leading an ignorant life of thinking that would never happen to me. I was on call for a doctor that was out on paternity leave, and got just unlucky enough that a brain-injury got called in while I was there. I was terrified, but something about seeing that poor man laying on the table when he came in, gave me all the confidence I needed to do my job with the professionalism that was expected of me. A few of the other doctors and nurses that were around kept saying that they were certain he would have brain damage, but my fresh eye to brain trauma proved otherwise. I ran several tests, even the ones not normally needed for that type of injury, and was able to conclude with certainty that, apart from a bad concussion, the man would be just fine.

That man was Kent, and when he came back to consciousness, mine was the first face that he saw.

"Are you the doctor that saved my life?" he asked.

"Well, I wouldn't say I had to save it," I responded. "It's a nasty injury, but fortunately you shouldn't suffer any brain damage. We'll keep you for a couple of days for observation, and then we'll monitor you closely for a couple of months after that. You'll need to check in regularly, and unfortunately, you're probably out for the remainder of the season." The Hellraisers weren't a Super Bowl team by any stretch of the imagination, but they were pretty good, so it was probably hard to hear that he'd be out for a while.

To my surprise, however, Kent started laughing. "Well, the girl I just started dating will certainly be pleased."

"That can't be true," I said. "If she really likes you, she won't be happy you're in pain." It made me slightly jealous to hear that he had a special someone. My job didn't allow time for dating, and even if it did, I wasn't actually all that great with women.

"No, she'll be very worried I'm sure. In fact…" A mischievous smile found his face. "I'm sure I can convince her to be my personal nurse."

I laughed. "Best of luck there."

"It's just that my job is very demanding, and I'm really close with a few of my teammates so she's always complaining I don't have enough time for her. She'll be thrilled that I have a medically mandated reason to take a break from playing and spend some time with her," he explained.

"I get that," I said. "Certainly I know what it's like to have a time-consuming line of work. Dating, doing anything fun, really relaxing of any kind are luxuries for me."

Kent's eyes got a little wider, and then squinted from the pain. "Ow."

"Yeah, don't do that," I said. "You'll really have to be careful about almost everything you do for a few weeks while this gets better."

"I just got excited because I thought of a way I can thank you," Kent said.

"There's no need to thank me, sir, I was just doing my job," I said, holding my hands up.

"Please," Kent said. "Even if you didn't have to save my life, as you say, you still helped me a lot and I really want to say thank you."

"I won't accept it," I persisted. "Really. It was my pleasure to be able to help you in any way I could."

"Then let me invite you out as a friend," Kent said. "You said so yourself, our jobs are alike, and you said you rarely get a chance to have fun and hang out. My friends are idiots, but why don't you come to our game with me on Sunday and then catch a beer with us afterwards? You may be a doctor, but you haven't lived until you've seen the way women hang on football players."

Despite my oath, and the fact that per the hospital regulations I was not supposed to accept gifts from patients except the odd small trinket, Kent's offer did sound really fun, and it just so happened that Sunday was an off day for me. The Texas Hellraisers were a big deal, and though I wasn't a football fan on the whole, I liked them as far as having a bit of hometown pride; it'd be cool to see them play in real life, and to actually hang out with someone other than my dog.

"As friends?" I asked.

"Of course, certainly not a thank you. I don't even think you did that great a job," Kent responded jokingly.

I nodded. "Okay, I'll take you up on that then."

The rest was history. I went to the game, they lost by four touchdowns, and then we drowned our sorrows in an inordinate amount of liquor. I met all of the guys in Kent's circle, including their true ringleader, Luke, who told me on the sly that if I was struggling with women he had a solution. He actually offered to share one of the women he was dating *with* me. He told me that, if I was interested, he thought I'd do well in their guy group because they shared many things, including partners. I wasn't really interested at first, it didn't seem like my cup of tea, but Luke convinced me and another non-believer of the group, Christian, to go to a swingers club with him. We met a woman there, a real bombshell, and she was willing to have sex with all three of us. They had dedicated rooms in the club for sex, and the three of us went to town on her. I liked it. I liked it a lot.

From then on, I was 'one of the guys' including being one of the ones they shared women with. We'd had sex in pairs, threes, even a few fours. I'd finally discovered a way to have a woman without the stress of keeping her satisfied with the crazy hours I worked. I could have her when I wanted, and had the other men to keep her happy when I wasn't available; it was a dream come true.

I walked into the bistro and smiled wider at Kent than I would have because I'd reminisced on the way over. I wouldn't say I was glad he got hurt, but I would say I was happy fate forced our paths to cross.

"What are you all smiley about?" Kent asked as I sat down.

"Just glad for the break from work. Thanks for inviting me," I said.

"Of course. I've had a taste for the brisket, and I know you love it here too. Plus, I wanted to hear from your lips, for certain, that you're not going to miss my wedding," he said.

I took a sip of my water. I eyed Kent's beer with

envy, but I was technically still on the clock. "I'm not going to miss your wedding, buddy," I assured. "I already got a doctor to be on call for me, the whole week. Her name is Dr. Jillian Portland, and I'm slightly concerned she's too good and is going to take my job."

I raised an eyebrow at Kent and he snickered. "What?"

"I was also told to take the night off for the bachelor party, so I sincerely hope you went with the rented out strip club I was promised," I said.

Kent nodded his head with a cheeky, perverted grin on his face. "Khloe made sure everything was all set."

I let out a loud bellow. "You made Khloe deal with arranging the strip club?"

"Of course!" Kent responded. "She's the wedding planner, and besides she demanded to make all the arrangements, even the bachelor/bachelorette parties. I mean, she nearly had an aneurysm when I told her we were renting out a strip club and they only accept payment in person, but she did it. She's a beast. If Luke isn't careful, she might run over him with her car."

I nodded; he wasn't wrong. "I wouldn't be surprised if she did, she's no pushover, and beautiful to boot."

It was Kent then that raised an eyebrow. "You're starting to sound like Luke."

"Don't insult me," I responded. "But, I'd be lying

if I said I wasn't attracted to her. I have been since the first time we met Khloe. Remember? When she chopped your groomsmen list down from fifteen to seven. All with the unlucky eight sitting right there."

"Just be grateful you made it," Kent said.

"Oh believe me, I am. She's given me a lot of wet dreams in the last couple of months. Sex with her would be a dream," I said.

"Join the club," Kent grumbled and my eyes went wide. He waved his hand through the air. "No, not me! I just mean I don't think you're the only one other than Luke holding a torch for her."

I raised an eyebrow. "Yeah?"

The waiter dropped our plates at the table and scuttled away. "Trust me," Kent said. "Every single one of my groomsmen is struggling to keep their paws off the wedding planner."

7

LUKE

THE BACHELOR PARTY

It was officially time for the only part of this stupid wedding that I was actually excited for; the bachelor party. Kent tried to sell me on some weak, 'boys night out, no stripper' bullshit, but I quickly put the kibosh on that. He had never allowed me to pull him into our fun with women, so I wasn't about to let him weasel out of a debaucherous, Luke-thrown bachelor party. I found the strip club in the city with the best reputation and demanded it be rented out for the night; all women included. It was going to be a booze-filled, butts and breasts shaking night of insanity, and I couldn't fucking wait. We decided to have it in the states before leaving for the island because Kent was intent on making sure Anna's big day wasn't ruined. Well, Kent… and Khloe.

"God, must you stand there buzzing like a child

high on sugar?" Khloe hissed when we all convened in front of the strip club at 6 o'clock sharp.

She wasn't pleased that she had to make a personal appearance to get us checked in on the big night, but I was plenty pleased to see her.

"I *am* a child high on sugar," I sang back at her, sashaying my hips and dancing to the thumping of music that could be heard booming from inside the club. I did a couple of pelvic thrusts towards her and she rolled her eyes.

"You're an ape," she snipped, then clapped her hands and turned her back to me, giving me a glimpse at her juicy, peach ass. "Alright. Gather round, gather round." All of the groomsmen and Kent gathered around Khloe, each of us laughing and rowdy, ready to get the party started. "Thank you for being here when I asked you. I'm glad you know your place, you're all very civilized." She pointed at me. "Except for this one, he's half-neanderthal."

I threw a hand down to cup my crotch. "You want a neanderthal, I'll give you a neanderthal."

There was a perk to Khloe's eyebrow that I caught, but I wasn't quite sure what it was. Part of me wanted to ask, but that would require not teasing her every waking moment and I wasn't really interested in that. I continued to wiggle my crotch in her direction until she finally let out a scoff of disgust and flipped me off, one of her bright, pink fingernails catching the light from the neon glow from the club.

"Thank you for proving my point," she growled. "I am perfectly disgusted to tell you all that the club is," she winced, "ready for your use. Silk, Candy, and Spice are all ready and excited to entertain you, but they wanted me to be sure and emphasize the fact that tips are *not* included in the cost of what was paid to secure the club, and that singles will not get you very far in an exclusive venue for the night."

Bram and Brett both raised their hands and in unison asked, "What's a single?"

Khloe rolled her eyes again and gave a few faux-claps. "Ha ha. Must be nice to be rich."

"It is nice," David said.

Khloe had to be developing a headache from the number of times she was rolling her eyes, but she looked adorable every time she did it. I couldn't keep myself from imagining her eyes rolling back in her head, not because she was annoyed with me, but because she was so enthralled with my dick ramming into her.

"I'm just about ready to let you loose, but first let me say—" Khloe's face settled into one of searing seriousness "—If any of you are late to catch the plane to this wedding, so help me god, I will personally see to it that your dicks are cursed and/or cut off. This wedding is about Anna, *not* you," she eyed me specifically.

"Loud and clear," I responded to her. "Anything else, mistress?"

Khloe sighed. "As much as I hate to admit it, my name is attached to this, so please don't embarrass me." She turned and groaned like she was about to take a party of six year olds into a McDonalds play place and started to trudge forward. "Let's go."

We all raced inside, and I intentionally stayed behind Khloe to watch her hips sway in the flowing skirt she was wearing. We entered and she stopped to talk to a woman dressed in a white button-up shirt, and a pair of tight short-shorts. She handed her an envelope and then shook her hand, and turned back around towards the door, jumping a little when she nearly ran into me.

"Well, I'm surprised you aren't in a boob sandwich right now," she hissed at me.

"The night's still young," I responded. "Besides, I'm an ass man."

Khloe gagged and then looked over her shoulder at the sound of resounding applause. One of the women was already topless and had Kent by the hand and was leading him into a private room and shutting the door.

Khloe shook her head. "This practice is barbaric," she turned back towards me, "and if he cheats on Anna, I'm holding you responsible."

"He's not gonna cheat on Anna. Believe me, I've tried to get him to," I responded.

Khloe's nose turned up into an entirely grossed out expression. "You are a *terrible* human being."

"I'll take that as a compliment." I took off my shirt and swirled it around above my head. Khloe pretended to be disgusted, but I could see her checking me out. Her eyes even danced with curiosity over the other guys as they floated around as well. "So, you came all the way out here. Why don't you let me buy you a drink?" I reached out and grabbed her hip and pulled her closer to me. "I'll make it worth your while."

Khloe snatched away from me, reeled her hand back, and slapped the dog shit out of me. It sent jolts of excitement straight to my dick. I wanted her more than words could say.

"Keep your hands off of me," Khloe murmured despite the bright red blush across her cheeks.

I chuckled evilly before risking it all to lean in and give her a kiss on the cheek, just barely managing to duck out of the way as she swung at me again, and made my way down to the join the guys and strippers.

Game, set, match, Khloe DuBois; you *will* pay for that slap.

8

KHLOE

As I watched the landscape of Texas disappear beneath the clouds, I began to wonder exactly where I had gone wrong in my life. Had I unintentionally pissed off some god or crossed fate poorly or somehow earned myself a steaming hot plate of bad karma? I'd planned everything so perfectly. I demanded that I be put in charge of booking the plane tickets so that I could intentionally situate myself as far away from the groomsmen as possible. In fact, I'd even sacrificed comfort to do so, placing myself in coach while all the guys were sitting up in first class, but wouldn't you know it, the person who was sitting next to me in my original seat had a baby with a special accommodation need. The airline was very apologetic for the mixup, and bumped me up to first class to meet the needs of the other passenger, and the flight attendant had a blush and a grin as she informed me

I was being moved to sit between two of the most attractive men she'd ever seen. Little did she know, they were also two of the biggest assholes on the flight, Luke Heath and Dr. Cody Williams.

Any other two groomsmen would have been sufficient. I could have held my own against David, Brett, Mason, Bram, or Christian, but Luke and Cody were the two groomsmen I hated the most. Luke was an extraordinary asshole, but Dr. Cody was in a league all his own. He went out of his way to make me feel small, insignificant and dumb. Every time he looks at me, my chest goes tight, and I can feel his judgment weighing down on me like a thousand bricks. It was going to be a miserable near 5-hour flight.

"Uh oh, doctor," Luke started as soon as I sat down. "The babysitter has arrived."

Cody looked down at me through his piercing, deep green eyes. "I suppose we had better be on our best behavior then, yes?"

I just ignored them. I shuffled myself into the seat between them, put my headphones in, and immediately went to ignoring them entirely. My brain went a little hazy and the intermingling smell of Luke's more sweet smelling cologne with Cody's dusky one. The flight attendant wasn't wrong by any stretch of the imagination. Luke and Cody were good-looking men; they were drop dead gorgeous. In fact, Kent's groomsmen were a veritable walking men's calendar. From the outside, they seemed like the perfect men, but in reality they were pretty presents with shitty gifts inside, but my eyes often betrayed me and sent the wrong message to my heart and... other parts of my body.

I slumped down in my seat as we flew along. From the corner of my eye I could see Luke and Cody literally talking over me, remaining engaged in heated discussion the entire time. I couldn't even imagine what the hell they could be talking about. Condescending or not, Dr. Cody was a *doctor*, and I distinctly remembered Luke struggling to fit square shapes into round holes. There was a rumor that he was secretly incredibly intelligent and just played dumb to seem more attractive to the idiot cheerleaders that didn't like to feel like the dumb one with the guys they were with, but I didn't buy it. It was much easier to accept that he was stupid and just really good at finding a few topics to be knowledgable about and hold the jerk doctor's attention.

Keeping my headphones in throughout the flight did seem to work, at first, keeping Luke and Cody from bothering me, but eventually, I noticed that Luke's eyes kept dropping down and painting over my body. I wasn't in anything too revealing, a pair of comfortable jogging pants and a long-sleeved t-shirt, but I still felt like he was undressing me in his mind. My body heated up as I remembered what Mason had told me at the grocery store a few days ago, mixed with Luke's behavior at the bachelor party. I'd planned to just write-off what Mason had told me, but ever since he'd said it, I had noticed that Luke's behavior seemed to match what he said. It wasn't as if it mattered, I wouldn't give Luke the time of day if he was the king of England, but he was easily the best-looking man that had ever been attracted to me, and that kind of thing elicits results regardless of my true feelings.

I reached into my bag and pulled out my face mask. It wasn't an incredibly long flight from Texas to Puerto Rico, but I could probably sleep through the rest of it and not have to deal with Luke's wandering eyes. I cranked up my music to try and truly pretend as if I wasn't in an asshole sandwich.

Before I put on my mask, I opened my phone to review the email that I had sent to my friend Jordan. She was still at my house when I had to leave for the plane, and I felt bad that I was leaving her alone. It worked out in an odd way, because I had free help to watch my house and feed my cat, but given what she was going through, I couldn't help but feel like I was abandoning her. I wrote her a very detailed email about everything she needed to know to care for the house, and I even agreed to let her go have some initial meetings with a client of mine as an assistant for some money. She'd have to figure out something else a little more permanent if she decided to stay, but she still wasn't sure what she was going to do.

Once I had suffered through enough anxiety about Jordan, I decided it was best I actually attempt to take a nap. I tried to stay focused on the music in my ears and drift off to sleep, but at least when I could see Luke and Cody I knew what they were doing, when I was blind to them, I was more unnerved. I was hoping to put them out of my mind, but eventually I made my peace with the fact that wasn't going to happen. I slyly tapped my smart watch with the pre-programmed motion to pause my music and decided to listen in on what the two of them were talking about.

"It's hard to think of you like that," Cody said. "Whenever we go out now, you're Mr. 'Every woman is beautiful. Their flaws are their strength,' blah, blah, blah."

Surely, Cody couldn't be talking about Luke; that didn't even sound like him. All women were beautiful? He once called me a 'Cheeseburger' to my face!

"I'm telling you man, I was a little fucking shit. All to impress some chick who couldn't even spell her own goddamn name. I was all caught up in being the jock with the head of the cheerleading squad girlfriend. I mean some of the stuff I did to her just because she wasn't some twig barbie doll was absolutely horrible. It's no wonder she hates me," Luke said.

I didn't know what to think. If he knew that the way he bullied me in high school was so awful, why was he still doing it? He teased me every chance he got.

"Are you sure it's cool to talk about her with her sitting right here?" Cody asked.

"Oh, yeah, she's out cold. Trust me. She used to hole up in the library back in high school and sometimes she would doze off. We..." Luke let out a deep, authentically sad sounding sigh. "We would draw on her face or take embarrassing pictures of her and she'd never wake up."

"Wow. That's cold," Cody responded.

"Yeah, it was," Luke said and goosebumps rose to my skin and how legitimately upset he sounded. "She didn't deserve any of that, even back then, but now I see what an amazing and beautiful woman she grew into. I'd probably let her kill me if she wanted to, and I'd go out happy."

"Dude, you've got it bad," Cody replied. "I mean, I get it, but Jesus."

"Tell me about it," Luke said.

Cody let out a sigh. "You like her. Like, for real."

Luke scoffed. "What? I'm just hot for her."

"Bullshit," Cody responded. "You used to notice her sleeping in her corner of the library? You and your friends spent a lot of time there?"

I shivered as Cody questioned Luke. What was he insinuating?

"I mean… It was the library," Luke said. "People needed to go there."

"All together as a group?" Cody asked.

"What the fuck is this? When did I start getting

interrogated? You're a nerd. You went to the library."

"Yeah, to study. Typically alone," Cody responded. "How many times did you go before your friends caught you spying on her?"

I was suddenly obscurely interested in the conversation. Did Luke... like me?

"Fuck off with your crazy theories. All I want from Khloe is that ass, that's it," Luke spat, but it wasn't entirely convincing. "I'd let her do literally anything to me. I wouldn't even stop her if she tried to choke me while we were having sex."

Cody snickered. "And when do you think that will happen?"

Luke scoffed, and I could feel him shift in his seat. "In my wildest dreams."

Cody murmured an affirmation and then conversation came to a halt. I sat there in total bewilderment for the remainder of the flight. Was Luke a totally different person from the man that I thought he was?

9

DAVID

I let out a hollow whistle as we walked through the lobby of the resort. It looked like a small city inside, with actual street signs pointing down different marble-clad hallways to get to the pool, the gym, the hotel rooms, and the beach, plus a special hall that led down to the ferry that would take us to the actual smaller island the wedding was on. The resort was directly on the water and the beach was only a hop, skip, and a jump away, and that was my number one goal; to check out the fine women that were certain to be enjoying a splash in the sun.

We checked into our hotel rooms, luxurious suites with two bedrooms, a kitchen, and living room, and I knew that if I could get a few gorgeous ladies back to see the view from the bay window, that I'd have no trouble at all getting into their pants. It had been months since I'd had sex of any kind, and thanks to Luke's infatuation with Khloe, he'd dragged our influx of shared women to a halt, so on top of ushering Kent through his important day, I had my own personal goal of ending my dry spell with some sexy, Puerto Rican women.

"This place is gonna be a honey trap," I said to Christian, my roommate for the trip.

"No kidding," Christian responded. "I can't wait to push a lady up against this window." He pushed against the glass as if checking to make sure it was durable. "Oh yeah, I'm gonna try and break it."

"If we work together, we can do it," I said with a laugh.

"Doctor's orders," Christian responded and held out a hand for a high-five. I slapped his hand and then we disappeared into our rooms to get comfortable and head out.

"I'm headed to the beach, man. You coming?" I called out.

"I'm gonna go meet up with Kent first, but I'm sure we'll make our way down there," Christian responded. "I gotta take a shower. I can feel the plane all over me."

I rolled my eyes. Christian was the 'pretty boy' of the group, so it made sense that he felt the need to bathe as soon as we got checked in. I wasn't that needy. Probably because I was constantly having to deal with sweat and grime on me as a football player, my threshold for needing to be pristine was much lower. I changed into my swim trunks and a t-shirt for traveling to and from, and made my way out of the room. As I left, my stomach growled with hunger, so I pit-stopped near the resort's fast food court. I picked up a veggie-burger and munched it as I made my way down to the beach.

The coastline was breathtaking. Despite the fact that it seemed like kind of a tourist location, the beach wasn't drenched with people, which was nice. It seemed as though the resort owned a private part of the beach, and only resort guests were on it. The crystal clear blue waters gently pushed against the light sand, filling the air with the calming sounds of wave against shore. It was a really beautiful place, I could even see myself getting married there someday. Just as I was thinking about the idea of even settling down, a flock of gorgeous women passed by me, reminding me that I wasn't ready to hang up my boots just yet. I started after them immediately, laughing when, as it turned out, I noticed I wasn't the only one hot on their trail.

"Hey! Get your own!" I looked over my shoulder and Luke, Brett, and Mason were walking up. Luke slapped his hand over my face as he got close enough. "We found these ones first."

"You act as if that's ever been an issue for any of us before," I responded.

"True indeed," Brett replied. He looked around the beach and then started applauding. "Yes sir, Puerto Rico is looking *mighty* nice."

"They're okay," Luke said with a lackluster dip to his voice.

Mason rolled his eyes. "Oh my god, we get it. Khloe's hot; you want her, but guess what? Unless you magically figure out how to turn into someone else entirely, it probably isn't going to happen. So pick up your dick and let's go find some women you actually stand a chance with."

Luke looked a touch dejected, but also seemed to be in agreement. We each lifted our shirts off our body and resumed trailing the works of pure art that had passed us by before. They weren't really trying to get away from us; in fact, all it took was catching up to them to engage them in some conversation. We brought them to the beach tiki bar and bought them some drinks and Mason floated the idea of getting together later on for some 'group fun.' They seemed interested, but seemed to have to ditch some of their wet blanket friends first and told us they'd give us a call later on. With the promise of some enjoyable company, the women left, leaving Luke, Brett, Mason, and I to talk and reminisce.

"I thought you were an idiot," I told Luke finally. "When you showed up on the field as a rookie, talking about 'baskets' and 'paddles,' I was certain you'd be traded out within the month."

When Luke first started, he played dumb, like he'd never actually played football before. He kept asking all the guys on the team what different things were and acting as if we were teaching him the game from scratch and he was just some kid who'd gotten lucky out of college. Turned out, he was the most sought after quarterback in the college circuit and that the Hellraisers had got lucky with a No. 1 draft pick that they traded with another team from the season prior.

"Out of everyone though, you were the most willing to help me," Luke said. "This fucking idiot," he slapped a hand on Mason's chest, "tried to get me dropped to third string."

"You called the goalpost a 'basket,'" Mason responded. "I wasn't about to have you hitting *me* in face with footballs."

"I was on board with third string," Brett said. "When you asked me what 'hut' meant, I was ready to punch you in your goddamn face."

After a lot of drinks and laughs, the sun began to set, and by that time Christian had called me to find out where we were to meet up. Christian, Cody, Bram, and Kent met up with us at the tiki bar and we continued drinking into the night.

"Hey guys," Kent started after a while. "I really promised myself that I wasn't going to get all emotional and sentimental, but getting married has a way of doing that to you."

I started to poke him and whine. "Awwwww."

Kent swatted my hand away. "I'm serious. I'll admit, I'm scared, but I love Anna and I can't wait to see what the future holds for us, but I know that I couldn't have done this without you guys. Having you all here… it really means a lot."

"To the groom," Cody said, holding up his cup.

"To the groom!" we resounded, and then everyone threw their cups together sloshing drinks around and even spilling some on the table.

"We're really the ones who should be thanking you," Luke said. "Not only is it an honor to be involved in your big day, but spending time on this island is amazing!"

Bram held up his cup. "To vacations on someone else's dime!"

We all tossed our cups together again, laughing as we cheered. "Hey, maybe tomorrow we should all have a huge game of beach football," Luke proposed. "If the doctor and the accountant can keep up."

"Don't you worry about me keeping up," Bram said. "You just worry about how you're going to explain that you lost a football game to an accountant."

"Damn! The gauntlet has been thrown down," I barked. "I wanna be on Bram's team."

Mason patted Kent's chest. "You in, Mr. Retired-and-Almost-Married?"

Kent nodded with a bright smile. "I'm down for sure. As long as you guys don't mind the girls tagging along. Anna told me she wants to get a tan for the wedding, so we were already planning on being on the beach tomorrow, Khloe included."

"I'll fucking drink to that," Luke said. He held his

empty glass in the air and a waitress walked over. She was skimpily dressed, wearing a black mini-skirt and a tankini that showed a lot of cleavage. "Can we get another round over here please?"

The waitress, a dirty blond with hazel eyes, smiled. "Of course, sir." She collected the empty glasses and was off a moment later.

Bram's eyes followed her closely as she walked away and then he tilted his head. "I'm a fan of the work uniform at this bar. Not to mention the workers."

"Yeah, they're pretty nice, but I'll say what we all know Luke is thinking," Cody interjected, "none of 'em holds a candle to Khloe."

Everyone agreed without question. I hadn't gotten to spend a ton of time with Khloe myself, but I knew she was sexy as hell; the kind of woman I typically went for. Some guys turn their noses up at meat on the bones, but I'd always preferred my women a bit thicker. Not only were they just more attractive to me than a woman that was skin and bone, but in my experience they were way better in bed. Gotta do something to make up for the fact that most guys go for skinny-minis, make sure they *want* to come back. Khloe had that syrup-bottle frame that made me want to pour *her* on a stack of pancakes. Large breasts and ass, a stomach with some substance, but still toned, and a nice pair of thick thighs that would feel good in my hands if I were holding her legs up. Just thinking about her got me hard. For a while, we were keeping it to ourselves that Luke wasn't the only one who had the hots for her, but it seemed like that cat was out of the bag.

"The real question is, Luke. Could you share?" I asked, knowing he'd carried the flame for her the longest.

"Are you kidding me? Half the times I've jerked off, I've imagined watching her get fucked by you guys." He closed his eyes and shook his head. "We shouldn't talk about it. I'll pop a boner right now."

Everyone laughed, but I held out my hands to quiet the table. "Okay, so then I think we need to set some ground rules."

"What do you mean?" Brett asked.

"Well, the key question," I continued. "If we *do* somehow luck into Khloe, do we up the ante on the scorecard?"

All of us, apart from Kent (except for one time when he was really drunk) had shared women throughout the duration of our friendship. It just worked best for all of us to work together keeping one woman satisfied rather than do it on our own, plus we found we were all freaks and liked to engage in types of sex far outside the norm. After we started to get a little bored with the typical run-and-gun with women, Christian invented 'The Scorecard.' It had all the different types of sex we liked to have; public, threesomes/foursomes, bondage, toys, sex with food, in a moving car, and orgies, and had them ranked in points by difficulty. The most point bearing thing on the card was 'the first' and it was for whomever could get our woman of choice to sleep with them first. Once we found a woman that we enjoyed, the game started, and it was up to each individual man to find a way to rack up the most points. The loser bought dinner for everyone at the nicest steakhouse in Austin; at least $2000 worth of food for the whole group. We didn't whip it out for every woman we shared, only the ones who seemed the most adventurous and exciting.

Kent let out a loud, exhausted sigh. "I fucking hate the scorecard."

"You're just a goody two-shoes," Mason spat. "Go ahead, Doc."

I nodded. "Thank you." I flipped Kent off before continuing. "First of all, dinner at Bottie's isn't gonna cut it for the winner of this card." There was a resounding sound of agreement. "Loser takes the entire group on vacation, all expenses paid."

"Out of the country!" Mason added.

I high-fived Mason and everyone laughed. "An international vacation, all-inclusive, courtesy of the loser," I reiterated.

"Take 'the first' off," Kent blurted out suddenly.

"What? Why?" Luke said. "That's the best one."

"Take it off because if you don't you're going to all be clamoring to get to her first and you're going to fuck up my wedding." Kent slammed his drink down on the table. "Let me make this perfectly clear. Khloe and I have gone to a lot of trouble to make this day perfect for Anna, and you seven aren't going to come in here being animals and ruin it. Khloe is *off limits* until we're wheels down in Texas and I'm off to my honeymoon. I'm not kidding. I won't talk to any of you again if you mess this up."

Luke held up his hands. "Whoa, whoa, whoa," he said. "Relax, it's not like we're actually going to try it or anything, it's just harmless fun. I'm sure you fantasized stuff like this about Anna. It's not like it's going to happen, but if by chance it does, we have something to work from."

"Damn right it's probably not going to happen. If you haven't forgotten, she can't stand you guys," Kent said.

I lifted my drink to my face, but muttered before I took a sip, "that should make the points for the first even higher."

"Yes!" Luke said, pointing at me excitedly.

"Take it off," Kent growled.

Luke shook his head. "We're not taking it off, but we solemnly swear we will not touch her, or even try, or even pretend to try, until after the wedding. Dr. Cody will you please prescribe Kent a double-dose of chill pills."

"I could, but that probably wouldn't do it," Cody said, and everyone laughed.

Kent started to loosen up once we assured him

that we would not do anything with Khloe until after the wedding, and we finished enjoying a couple more rounds of drinks, and then retired to our rooms for the night. Just before falling asleep, we got a group message from Luke. It included a picture of the scorecard he drafted, alongside a text:

I don't know if any of you jacked off to the thought of doing this with Khloe, but I know I did. Let the games begin.

10

KHLOE

"Khloe, pleeeeeease?" Anna was standing in my hotel room trying to convince me to go sunbathing with her despite the fact that I was just sitting with her and Kent at breakfast when he mentioned that all the groomsmen would be on the beach today. "It'll be fun, and I'll be bored with all the guys playing and Kent ignoring me."

"Just like the good ol' days," I spat back, not intending to be as mean as I sounded. Anna poked out her bottom lip and I knew I'd dug myself a grave. "I'm sorry, that was mean, but I'm really looking forward to *not* having to deal with the guys today."

"So don't deal with them," Anna responded. She looked so innocent with her pixie haircut, and her eyes glowing in the morning sunlight streaming in through the window, it was hard to deny her; like a little kid asking for candy. "Kent said he made them promise to lay off you last night because it's almost the wedding day, plus we'll look so good with nice island tans in the wedding photos." She grabbed my arm and pulled. "Please? It's my wedding."

I sat there looking at her in disdain before finally letting out a sigh. "Fine."

Anna jumped up. "Yes! It's gonna be great." She ran into the bathroom and when she came back she had a towel in her hands. It was wrapped in an orange bow and had my name on it. "Here."

I took it with a smile, but a slight tilt to my head. "I think the resort supplies towels."

"Just open it," Anna whined.

I undid the bow and unfurled a towel and a peach bathing suit fell out. The bottoms had a cute ruffle around the waist and the top had an 'M' on the right cup and an 'H' on the left cup, and they were attached with a silver clasp that looked like an 'O' so when looking at it it had the initials 'MoH' for 'Maid of Honor.' The towel was white and had letters scrawled across that read, 'I'm with the bride' and when I looked back up at Anna, she'd opened her sundress to reveal her matching bathing suit that 'BtB' for 'Bride to Be' on it, and held up her towel that said, 'I'm the bride.' It was adorable.

"Oh my god," I said. "This is too cute. I can't."

Anna nodded. "I know! Aren't you glad you agreed to come?"

I laughed. "That remains to be seen, but I do love these." I hugged her. "Thank you."

"No, thank you," she responded, then she pushed me away. "Now go change so we can hit the beach!"

I did exactly that. I skipped into my bathroom and put on the new bathing suit that Anna got me, feeling a little arrogant at how cute it looked on me. The bottoms hugged my wide hips perfectly, and the ruffles brought attention to my full thighs, that I was actually a big fan of. The top struggled to contain my breasts, but in a way that was teasing and fun, and despite the fact that I was a bigger girl, my belly was flat and toned, so I didn't mind going out in a bikini top. If Luke really did find me attractive, he was going to eat his heart out. I pulled on a pair of shorts and one of my loose, yarn shawls that I always wore to the beach, and then Anna and I headed out.

When we got down to the beach, the game of beach football that Kent had told Anna and I would be happening was already underway. Many of the resort guests had gathered around and were watching the game, and it wasn't hard to see why. All of the guys glistening with sweat, with their abs revealed to the world and their calves working overtime to grip the loose sand as they ran around and tackled one another; they were a treat for the eyes for sure. Kent fit right in among the good looking men, with his feathered, light brown hair, perfectly sculpted body, and deep dimples, and the eight of them simply looked good doing what they did best.

"Damn, my husband is sexy," Anna hissed.

"Yeah, yeah, you're very lucky," I replied. "Put lotion on me."

We found a spot near enough to the game to watch, but far enough away to not be sucked into the crowd, and put our towels down. Once we were comfortable, we took out the suntan lotion and took turns helping one another apply generous coats.

"So," Anna asked as she massaged some across my back. "How's it going with these guys? I know you hate them and you're only tolerating them for me, but are things getting *any* better?"

"What about the way those men behave would make you think they'd get better for any reason?" I responded. "You were the one that told me that they were uncivilized and awful."

"I know," Anna responded, "but you're so great. I guess I assumed you'd soften them up."

She wasn't entirely wrong. I couldn't stand them, but after hearing Luke and Cody talk on the plane a couple of days prior, it was clear I'd had some sort of profound affect. "I'm just holding onto my few remaining threads of sanity. This process with them has been trying."

Anna whimpered. "I'm sorry. I didn't mean for my wedding to stress you out."

I whipped around and grabbed Anna's hands.

"No! I'm so glad I got to do this for you. I wouldn't give it up for anything in the world. I'd deal with these men for another six months for you."

Anna smiled. "Thank you, you're a good friend."

"Besides," I said, squeezing some lotion onto my hands and rubbing it onto Anna's back. "It isn't just because of them. I also had a friend come to stay with me for a while. She's having a tough time back home."

"Oh no," Anna said.

"Yeah," I said. "Her name is Jordan. Believe it or not, she's in love with six men."

"*Six?!*" Anna yelped. "I can barely handle one."

I laughed and she joined me. "I know."

I decided to keep it to myself that I'd considered that type of relationship on more than one occasion. I opened my mouth to say something else, when I was interrupted by a voice singing at me from across the beach.

"Oh, mistress!" I rolled my eyes at the sight of Luke leading all seven men in my direction, still shirtless, still glistening, still mouthwatering, still assholes.

I dug my foot into the sand and prepared to take off. "Bye."

Anna grabbed my arm and held me in place. "No! You said you were going to sunbathe with me. Just ignore them. What was that you just said? You'd deal with them for another six months for me?"

I glared at Anna and rolled my eyes. "Bitch."

"Love you too," Anna responded.

I pulled my sunglasses from the top of my head where they had been sitting, down over my eyes, and tried to lay back and relax, but my body was tied in more knots than a sailor's rope. All those good-looking men headed straight at me, my groin was tingling just imagining two or three of them having their way with me.

I shook the lurid thoughts from my mind as Kent ran interference to try and keep the guys out of our hair. I could overhear him telling them that we were trying to tan and that if they knew better, they'd avoid us. I took out the notebook I'd brought with me to the beach and started double checking that I had everything in line for the wedding. The videographer was all set up to tape it for Anna and Kent's families back home. Cece said the flowers would be arriving 24 hours before the wedding. I'd already called to confirm the venue was ready, and I would be able to get in the night before to make sure it was decorated appropriately. I'd spoken with the caterer who was already on the island and ready to prepare the perfect tropical food for Anna's ideal day. The groomsmen…

I looked up and saw the groomsmen all eyeing me from where they were standing by Kent.

…the groomsmen were all there, and that was probably going to be the biggest problem I'd have to face.

11

CODY

I was feeling good from our first game of beach football and was ready to get into game two. It was a beautiful day on the beach, with the sand not too hot that it couldn't be walked on, but still warm enough that it felt good on my bare feet as I charged through it. My calves were on fire from fighting against the malleable sand, but I knew that it was only strengthening them for my favorite past-time of running.

All the guys were gathered up and ready to get a second game going, but we'd reached something of an impasse. The game was *fun*, but we were all inherently competitive guys, and just playing for shits and giggles wasn't enough to really get our blood pumping. Some of the beach goers had gathered around to watch us play against one another, but it still didn't really feel like the stakes were high enough.

"A hundred dollars?" David suggested for a bet.

"That's chump change for us," Brett replied.

"A thousand?" Mason said.

I shook my head. "It's not money. That's not what we need to bet. It needs to be something else."

"Well what? Booze? A car?" Bram said. "I can't think of anything besides money."

We stood there in silence for a minute all trying to put our minds on what we could bet to make the game more interesting. We were a very tight knit group and shared a lot of things, so most of our material property was always at one another's disposal. I knew that we had to bet something high profile to make the game worth playing, but I couldn't wrap my mind around what that item would be. I started to look around the beach, hoping that maybe something one of the guests had on them that would help me figure it out, when my eyes found the perfect thing.

Not too far from where we were playing, sunbathing on a towel, with her milky skin shimmering in the sun, was Khloe. I zeroed in like a crosshairs through a scope. Damn she was lovely. She was perfect as far as I was concerned. As a doctor, I was well aware of what a good, healthy woman looked like, and Khloe was it with a cherry on top, or should I say it with two big, voluptuous breasts on top and a pert, apple ass on the bottom. Most women weren't good-looking enough to make me blink when they passed by, but Khloe was enough to make me stop and look twice.

I glanced over my shoulder just in time to see Luke's jaw clench and eyes pierce, almost as if he was angry, but I knew he was trying to keep his arousal in check; weren't we all? It didn't help that we'd indulged ourselves in a conversation about actually getting Khloe; it had probably made things much worse for everyone. Still, something interesting caught my eye as I turned my head to take another drink of Khloe's form. Despite her best attempts to seem like she wasn't, every few seconds her eyes would drift up and land on Luke. It did make me briefly jealous that he was the one drawing her attention, but I couldn't necessarily blame her. I didn't need to be a woman to see that Luke was a Greek god. He had chiseled, toned abs, and well-defined biceps. He'd been considered for a popular magazine's yearly 'Most Attractive Man of the Year' award, just barely losing out to a world-renowned actor. Bram and Brett were near the top of the pack too, but even I could see they had nothing on Luke. He was gorgeous, and if Khloe was going to give in to any one of us, it was likely to be him.

That's when it hit me. Khloe was the bet.

I was fully aware of the fact that we were crossing over from demeaning with the scorecard to straight up pigs offering her as a bet, but if we were going to do it, why not go all in? I pulled Luke a few feet away from the guys, mostly Kent, and lowered my voice.

"I know what we're gonna bet," I said. "Gotta keep it from Kent though."

Luke didn't look crazy about the idea. He was Kent's best friend and the best man at his wedding, so it probably made him a little uncomfortable to keep something from him. After contemplating it for a few seconds, however, he peeked over his shoulder at Kent and then nodded an affirmation at me.

"The winner gets to make the first move on Khloe," I said.

Luke let out a dramatic gasp. "You wanna bet 'The First?' We can't do that."

"Scared you're gonna lose?" I teased. "This is your job, right? Surely you'll have no problem beating me."

Luke's face got a little red. Whether or not he was planning on maintaining his promise to Kent to not touch Khloe until after the wedding, he'd prob-ably already decided that he'd be the first one. In truth, I wasn't actually planning on beating Luke and winning the right to go for her first, but I wasn't going to just roll over and let him take it; if we wanted something interesting to bet, this was certainly it.

"What about the rest of the guys? We can't all bet it if we're playing in teams," Luke said.

"We'll play three games. First four versus four.

The winning team splits into two teams, each team gets two of the losers, and we play again. The two guys on the winning team from the second round, who also won the first round, become captains, the captains pick teams for the final round, and we duke out. The winning captain gets to ask out Khloe," I explained. "Easy."

"'Oh, look at me. I'm a doctor. I'm good at math,'" Luke mocked.

"You have a business degree," I growled at him. "Quit stalling and man up," I said.

Luke peeked back at the guys, then over at Khloe, then back at me. "How do we tell the other guys without telling Kent?"

I clapped my hands and turned around and walked over to Kent. "Hey, Kent."

Kent turned around and looked at me. "Yeah? Are you two about done making out over there?"

"Hilarious," I said flatly, just as Luke was making his way over as well. "Luke and I thought it might shake things up to do things tournament style. Each of us pitches in $50 and the winner gets $400."

"How will only one person win?" Kent asked.

"A three game style where the winners keep splitting teams until we're down to two. I'll explain it all, but it'll be easier if I can write it out on a piece of paper." I pointed over to where Khloe and Anna were sitting, feeling a bit of internal pride at the way Khloe jumped and turned her head away the second I did it. "Since we're not allowed to go near

Khloe, can you go ask to borrow a piece of paper and a pencil?"

"We could just keep score on our phones like we did the first game?" Luke said. I turned and looked at him and sighed. For an incredibly intelligent man, he could be really thick. He stared back at me for a moment and his eyes widened. "Oh, right, you're a doctor so you prefer shittily writing things out."

Kent snickered. "Good one." He fist bumped Luke and then turned and rushed off towards Khloe and Anna.

When he was close enough to the women, Anna jumped up to kiss Kent and I knew he'd be distracted for a couple of minutes. I gathered the rest of the guys and explained my plan. Even though everyone was still trying to be somewhat solicitous of Luke being the first one to lust after Khloe, it didn't take much to get them on board. Everyone was fired up to compete for the challenge to be Khloe's first of the seven of us, or at least to be the first one shot down. It kicked the fire into us all that we needed to make the football games high stakes and adrenaline fueling. I explained that everyone was going to have to ante up $50 bucks if for some reason Kent won, but it was a small price to pay for the chance to go after Khloe.

Once Kent got back with the paper and pen from Khloe, I explained the modified rules to him, we decided we would play to 18 and then wrote out the brackets. The first round teams were decided completely at random. I used the bottom of the paper we got from Khloe to write all of our names on, and then let a couple of the onlookers draw two names from a hat for captains. Each captain then drew names randomly until we had two teams of four. Kent was the captain of the first team and drew Mason, Brett, and David, and Luke was captain of the second team and drew me, Bram, and Christian. A coin toss determined that Kent's team was the receiving team and the game was underway.

It became clear fairly quickly that the teams were pretty mismatched. Even though Luke got saddled with the two "non-ballers" of the group, me and Bram, we worked together with Christian and Luke so well, that you wouldn't know we weren't professionals. Toss in the fact that Mason and David were used to working with Luke as the quarterback, so trying to play with Kent who was traditionally a defensive player was a bit of a struggle. We were more agile, younger, and more adept, and the match ended in a complete slaughter; 18-0.

For the next round, we followed a similar system. A guest watching us play picked two names at random to be captains, and then each of them picked one name at random from the remaining two winners. The captains then had their pick of the losers to round out their teams. The captains pulled were Christian and me, and Christian pulled

Bram, which left me with Luke. Luke and I had gotten close over the course of our friendship and I was confident we could pull out a second victory, plus it would be delightful irony for it to be he and I in the final matchup.

Christian picked Brett and David for his team, which was just plain rude. It wasn't as if Mason and Kent were bad at the game, but they were the 'old cats.' I was technically older than them both, but Kent was retired and a bit out of practice, and Mason was notably slower. Luke seemed thrilled to end up with them, however, and after we got into the game it was clear why. I was too fast, Mason was too big, and Kent was too smart. It didn't matter what we decided to do. If we needed to throw it, Kent could be downfield in an instant, and if we needed to just charge through, Mason had the girth to make it happen. I ran feints most of the game, but it worked because I was always able to fool at least the accountant and leave one person open for Luke to work with. It was a closer game, but in the end, Luke and I ended up snagging our second victory 18-12.

"Alright, it's all down to you two," Kent said. "Luke, you're a superstar, man. My money's on you."

"I don't know," Mason said. "The good doctor is the big shock of the day. Who knew med school prepared you so well for a pump fake!"

We all laughed, and then Luke stuck out his hand. "May the best man win."

I took Luke's hand in my own and he squeezed it until it felt like he was going to shatter my bones. His pupils were dilated like a man on drugs, and the sweat and grime on his body was radiating like an aura of strength. Suddenly, I was feeling like I'd made a mistake dangling Khloe in front of him like a well-seasoned steak; he was borderline feral.

"Good luck to you," I responded.

Luke released my hand, and pulled a coin from his pocket and handed it to Kent. "Flip for picks." He tilted his head at me. "You call it."

I chuckled. He was in another world. "Fine." Kent tossed the coin in the air and the second it left his hands I made my call. "Heads." The coin dropped back into Kent's palm and he flipped it to the back of his other hand. He lifted up to reveal the coin which was heads-side up. I smiled. "We'll kick first."

Luke shook his head. "That flex is gonna cost you, doctor."

And he was right. With my chosen team of Kent, Brett, and Christian, we were no match for Luke, Mason, Bram, and David. They were a well-oiled machine. Even with Bram the accountant, it was as if he'd been playing football with the others his entire life. After a game like the one he played, he could stand to be drafted. It was like there were twelve of them out there. Every time I looked up, someone else was running circles around me, and I was ashamed to say, it was another total blowout.

Luke was the cornerstone to it all, and as the sun started to descend towards the horizon Luke took home the third and all around victory. Call it poetic justice, but he'd earned himself the right to make the first move on Khloe.

"Yes!" Luke shouted. He pointed directly at me and stuck his tongue out. "Yes!" He started to leap around like a monkey. "I guess that's why I'm the goddamn quarterback, boys! Football extraordinaire!" He stopped and stuck his nose in the air and screwed his face as though he was trying hard to calculate something. "How many wins was that? How many times did I lose?" He put his hands on his hips in a superhero pose. "Oh, right. Three wins for me, zero losses. Suck it!"

"You're a tool." Brett hissed.

Luke stuck up his middle finger. "You're just mad that you lost."

"That's true," David said, but then he turned his finger to Luke, "and you're a tool."

We decided to dip our feet in the water to counteract the steaming Puerto Rican heat. As we were all sitting at the edge of the water cooling off and refueling after a series of hard-fought games, Kent walked over to visit with Anna and Luke decided to get in a little bit of friendly gloating.

"If I so much as see one of you look at her before I get a chance, I'm opening up a can of whoop ass," Luke said.

"But we're sticking to the promise not to touch her until after the wedding, right?" Bram asked.

"We have to," I said quickly. "Especially if we're really going to let Luke go first, he's the one most likely to cause problems."

"Hey, I resent that," Luke said. "It's true, but I resent that."

"He's not gonna go for it anyway," Brett said, with everyone's heads flying to him in shock. "After all this time, if he hasn't shot his shot, he ain't gonna."

I looked over at Luke and his head looked like it was about to burst and deflate like a cartoon. He looked back at Khloe, and then over at Brett, and I could see the gears turning. I didn't know what he was planning, but I was instantly afraid of it. Finally, as if something had just kick started his engine, he jumped up from the edge of the beach, bolted over to Khloe, snatched her up out of her spot, and threw himself and her both into the ocean.

"Uh oh," I said, joining all of the other guys in dropping my jaw. "That's not good."

12

KHLOE

I didn't even have time to react. One second, I'm laying on my towel, taking in the beautiful, Puerto Rican sun, and then next second I had been lifted from my spot and was rushing towards the water against my will. The moment seemed to slow for a moment as I tried to figure out what was going on. I could see six of the groomsmen off to one side, with their feet in the water, all staring at me with their jaws dropped. I could see Kent and Anna back by where we were laying, both also with looks of total shock on their face, and there were a few other people on the beach hooting and hollering in my direction. Finally, I looked up and saw Luke's face, pursed and determined, as my captor and before I could even open my mouth to scream, I was totally submerged in the cool ocean, tasting as the saltwater rushed up my mouth and nose.

I flailed about until I could find my footing and then I stood up. My hair clung to my body, drenched in water and I gagged trying to get the water free of my throat. Luke's hands were still all over my body, holding me in the water, and as I finally started to come to my senses, the only thing I could think to do was swing. I barreled out my arm towards Luke's face, but he caught it and held it firmly in place.

"Fuck!" I barked. "Let me go you fucking asshole!"

"Calm down," Luke said. "It's just water."

"My hair is soaked, I'm going to have to do it again, you dick," Khloe hissed.

"Lighten up, Mom. I was just trying to have some fun," Luke replied with an insidious laugh.

I swung out again, making hard contact with Luke's chest. I pulled my hand away to see a bright red outline of palm forming where I'd hit him. I was hoping that would be enough to get him to let me go, but he just chuckled. He used his hold on my other hand to pull me closer to him, and beneath the surface of the water, his other hand coiled around and took a huge fistful of my ass.

He brought his mouth near my ear and his hot breath tickled my chilled neck. "I want you."

I tried to ignore the heating of my body. I tried to pull away, but he held me close. Time seemed to move a little slower. For a moment, I got lost in what was happening. Luke was attractive and being in the water, with the heat bearing down us, and his hands on my body, I started to slip. I relinquished control for a moment, and Luke's hand on my ass gripped a little tighter.

I looked up and my eyes locked into Luke's and I remembered where I was, and more importantly who I was with. What the hell was I doing? I brought my knee up towards Luke. I was hoping for a groin shot, but I wasn't able to get enough inertia in the water, and I just ended up pushing him away with my knee. As he moved a few inches back, I swung my hand at his face and slapped him right across the cheek.

"Stay away from me, psycho," I growled. I started to march out of the water, but Luke grabbed my arm again and pulled me back. I glared over my shoulder at him. "Let go."

"If you want me, and I know you do, come find me in my room later. I know you know which room I'm in," Luke said.

I snatched my arm away from him and made my way out of the water and up the beach to where my items were sitting. I started gathering up all of my things, despite feeling Kent and Anna's eyes on me.

"Khloe," Anna started, but I shook my head.

"I'm sorry," Kent said. "I really did tell him to lay off."

"He doesn't understand normal, human language," I explained. I looked at Anna. "I'm sorry. I gotta go. My hair is going to be a ball of frizz any moment."

"I understand," Anna said.

I didn't wait for any additional go-aheads. I didn't look back at the other guys, I certainly didn't look back at Luke, I just grabbed up all of my stuff and stormed away. I was shaking with anger as I made my way through the resort hallways and up to my room. The nerve of that asshole. Not only did he drag me into the ocean water, ruining my tan and messing up my hair, but then he had the nerve to just help himself to handful of my ass and whispers that he wants me? Who the fuck did he think he was? If I did go and see him it would only be to kick his ass, and nothing else.

I blasted into my room and tossed my things onto the bed. I made my way into the bathroom, stripped off my drenched bathing suit, and then ran a shower. I turned the water until it was almost too hot to bear and then climbed in, letting it splay over my body and, hopefully, wash the salt from my hair. I stepped out briefly to grab my comb, and started the slow process of feeding it through my hair to try and get it clear of the salt water that was already tangling it. It was going to be a process. Saltwater and my hair did not mix very well, so it would take an additional wash sometime later on, but once my comb was sliding through unhindered, I decided it was good enough for the time being. I slathered in some shampoo and washed it through a few times, and then did the same with some conditioner. When my hair was clean, I turned to washing off my body, scrubbing well, almost as if I could wash away the tingling remains of Luke's hands on my skin.

I put him out of my mind, turned off the shower, and got out. I didn't put any clothes on for the moment, and instead just slipped on the hotel robe and climbed into bed. I grabbed the menu sitting by the phone, picked up the receiver and ordered room service. I was trying not to run up Kent and Anna's wedding bill any more than I needed to, and I was in a constant battle to break my habit of stress-eating, but I think all parties involved would agree I'd earned myself a room-service steak and potatoes. Once I'd had a chance to eat and calm down, I turned my attention back to double checking the details for the wedding and making sure everything was in line, apart from the fact that I angrily scratched out Luke's name any time it appeared on the paper.

I exhausted all of the things I could do inside my room and finally became bored. It was in a beautiful tropical location, and thanks to an asshole who's been haunting me for ten years, I was holed up in my room? No. I got out of bed, changed into one of my comfortable dresses, slipped on my flip flops and left the room. I didn't know what I was going to do, but it was a refreshing, chilly island night and I was desperate to enjoy it.

"Miss?" I'd wandered down into the lobby and must have looked lost enough to elicit help from the staff. A concierge in a tropical shirt and navy slacks was walking over to me. "Can I help you find something?"

"Sure," I responded. "I'm bored and just looking for something to do. I don't want to travel too far away from the resort, and if it sounds like it would attract a group of gorgeous, idiotic men, do *not* send me there."

"Uh, okay," the concierge replied. "Well, if you're just looking to have a drink—"

I cut him off before he could finish. "A drink sounds good."

He chuckled. "Well then you should visit our state of the art tiki bar. I believe I recognize you from the wedding that's in this week, correct?"

"Yes," I responded.

"Then you should have two drinks comped to your room, given you haven't used them yet," the concierge explained.

"Free drinks?" I asked. "Yes, sir, I will take that please."

The concierge pointed down one of the hallways. "Head down this way like you're headed to the beach, and you'll see the resort entrance to the bar on your left. It's got a beautiful balcony where you can enjoy the fresh air and our tiki lamps which burn in a variety of colors."

I nodded. "Perfect. Thank you so much."

I pulled a $5 bill from my clutch and slipped it to the concierge and then followed his directions to make my way to the tiki bar. I walked into the bar and was immediately blown away. It was beautiful inside. There were dangling white lights lining all of the banisters, and the roof was faux-thatch like an old hut. About halfway through the bar, it transitioned to a gorgeous deck that was completely exposed to the stunning night. Stars dotted the sky and the sounds of the uninterrupted waves crashing against the shore filled the air amidst the absent chatters of the guests inside. Surrounding the balustrade enclosing the deck, were a variety of tiki torches that all burned brightly in flames of pink, green, blue, red, and purple; it was astounding.

There was one circular bar that was designed so that half of it sat inside the establishment and the other half sat outside. I knew I wanted to enjoy the night sky, so I made my way out to the outer bar. I walked up to the counter and a bartender walked over, his eyes lighting up as he looked over me.

"Well, hello there," he greeted. He had caramel skin and slicked back black hair. He was no Luke, but he was good-looking.

"Hi," I responded. "I'm looking for something fruity and strong."

"Absolutely. One Island Sunrise, coming up," he replied. I showed him my ID and then he flitted away.

"I'm on my third Island Sunrise. I think you'll

enjoy it." My heart sank and my skin crawled. I slowly turned my head to the right, and it became clear that the gods had teamed up to smite me. Luke was sitting at the bar, a few feet away from me, working on a drink in a pineapple. We locked eyes and he smiled. "Hey."

"Fuck my life, I knew I should have stayed in my room," I responded. "You are a tumor."

Luke winced a little. "Ouch, that was harsh. I didn't realize you were so averse to water."

"I'm not averse to water, I'm averse to being dragged into water against my will by men that I can't stand," I hissed back. "Now please leave me alone."

"Look, I'm sorry, or whatever," Luke said. "Kent ripped me a new one for messing with you, so I'm sorry."

"You know when 'I'm sorry' sounds really sincere? When you explain that someone forced you to say it and add 'or whatever' to the back," I said. "I don't care. If you're sorry even a little bit, just stop. We only have a few more days to deal with each other and then we never have to see each other again, so just… just stop." My throat started to burn. The last thing I wanted was to show Luke any sign of weakness, but years of being tortured by him was boiling near the surface threatening to bubble over. "You've been a jerk to me my entire life, and I don't even know what I did to deserve it. Why? Just because I was a little chubby? Do you have any idea at all how difficult it was to get through those four years? High school is supposed to be the best time of your life, but thanks to you, it wasn't for me."

Luke frowned. "Khloe."

"No, just… For once, listen instead of talk." I turned to face him outright so that he understood the seriousness tensing my body as I spoke. "I hate you, and there's nothing else to it. You made those four years miserable for me and now it's ten years later and you're still doing the same thing. Please, if there is even part of you that is human at all, just leave me alone. Be a civilized human being for once and let me get through these next few days without any additional pain." The bartender set down the drink and slinked away, sensing that the conversation was not one he should interrupt. I picked it up and turned my back to Luke to walk away. "Goodbye."

As I was walking away, I felt someone grab my wrist. I looked over my shoulder and Luke immediately pulled his hand away. "I'm sorry." There was a sincerity in his eyes that I had never seen before. It was enough to keep me there to hear what more he had to say. "Seriously. I'm sorry. Not just for today, but for all of it. I was an ass back in high school. No, more than an ass, I was unworthy of being in your presence, let alone making it so difficult for you." My skin prickled with warmth as I listened to his words paired with how honest he seemed. "I was an idiot kid who thought I knew what would make me happy, but instead it made me miss out on this really amazing person that, honestly, I probably would have really loved to get to know back in the day. And now she's standing in front of me and I have this crazy opportunity to not repeat the mistakes of my past, and what am I doing? I'm being the same idiot I was back then. Seriously, from the bottom of my heart, I'm sorry. For everything." He smiled. "And for what it's worth, I thought your hair looked good wet. I also think it looks good now."

I stood in silence. I wasn't expecting such a passionate, heartfelt apology. I had no idea how to respond. What was worse, is that his language, demeanor, everything was totally different from the Luke I was used to. He sounded kind, intelligent, and considerate; nothing like the asshole I'd had to endure for the past six months or the past ten years. He was unbelievably sexy, and if he was actually a good guy; that changed everything. I couldn't wrap my mind around it.

"I accept your apology," I murmured. I couldn't shake the feeling that I needed to leave immediately. The longer I stood there, the more risk I ran of losing control. "I'm gonna go."

I turned around again, still entirely unsure of what was going on in my brain. How could a single apology change my perception so much? I'd just told him I hated him five minutes prior.

I grabbed my drink and started to amble away when his dusky voice filled my ears again. "I do want you, you know?" It stopped me dead in my tracks. "I've been lusting after you for a long time now; six months, right? Since the second I laid eyes on you again."

I rotated back again and stared deep into his azure eyes. "I know," I said.

"You know?" he said. "So, where does that leave us?"

13

LUKE

I watched Khloe carefully for signs of her response. There was a slight shake to her legs and a few beads of sweat had pooled at her hairline. She was nervous, but the way her pupils flared told me she was also excited. I stood up from my stool and walked over to her. I threaded my fingers into her hair and around until my hand was cupping the back of her head. I leaned in until my lips were perched just in front of hers, and then teasingly passed them by, situating my lips near her ear.

"I've been told I'm barred from touching you because I have a way of fucking things up, and Kent is hellbent on making sure this wedding is perfect for Anna." I pressed my lips to the soft skin of her cheek and the scent of her honey shampoo burst into my nose. I was at the cliff's edge about to jump. "But I can keep a secret, if you can."

I could feel Khloe trembling in my grip, and if I had my way, it was just the beginning of the way I wanted to shake her. Her hands tentatively gripped my sides. "This may be the worst decision I ever make, but…" I looked down into her chocolate eyes and I knew in that instant that I had her. "Fuck me," she said, and it was like absolute music to my ears.

I pulled Khloe back against a difficult to see corner of the bar and pinned her against the wall. I placed my lips on her neck and sucked wildly, loving the taste of her skin as it sunk into my mouth.

"It's not just me that wants to fuck you," I whispered into her ear as I slid my hand down her torso and snaked it up her dress. "All of the guys do." I threaded my fingers under the fabric of her underwear and started to rub at her heated and already moistening pussy. She gasped into my ear as her body trembled under my touch. I laced the lips of her vagina with my finger, sawing gently against her clit and hole. "I'm gonna fuck you, and then I want to watch my guys fuck you. One of them in this tight pussy, and the other one in your beautiful ass."

I nibbled Khloe's bottom lip and she mewled into my mouth. Her hands shook, gripping onto my shoulders for balance. She didn't know the trouble she was in. We were still in Act I. I started to increase the pace fingering her, continuing to kiss her peach lips, and breathing in the sound of her moaning into me. In no time at all, she was grinding her own hips against my hand, fucking herself on my fingers. I pulled my hand back when I sensed she was about to cum and she let out a whine of frustration.

"Not too fast," I told her. I unbuttoned my pants and then kissed her again, placing a hand on her head. "I want you to suck me now." I placed pressure on the top of her head, and she gave way, dropping down in front of me.

With a few quick motions, she had my cock free of my pants and boxers, and I knew I wasn't working with an ordinary animal. She took my rock hard dick into her hands and stroked it a few times before looking up at me with her beautiful doe eyes, and slipping my leaking shaft into her mouth. Khloe on her knees, with my dick in her mouth and her eyes locked in mine, while the heat of her mouth enveloped me; it was sin that I was experiencing it for free. I kept my gaze on her as she moved her mouth up and down, taking more and more of me in with each bob.

I brushed my thumb over her cheek. "That feels so good."

Khloe winked at me, she actually winked at me, and I felt like I was going to bust right then and there. She was a wolf in sheep's clothing. I had my dick in her mouth, but she was letting me know in no uncertain terms that it was she who was in charge. She slurped around me with fervor, finally dropping her eyes from mine to focus on the task at hand, and I let my head lull backwards and my eyes drift shut. Khloe's tongue coiled around my cock, strangling it, and attempting to milk it for all it had. The feeling was unlike any I'd ever had before, and the couple of functioning brain cells I had remaining couldn't wait to share the feeling with my friends.

I reached down and grabbed her arm and pulled her to her feet. I threw my mouth against hers, sucking her tongue into my mouth, and humming along with her as we connected. I took her ass into both of my hands and squeezed, and knew that I didn't want to wait any longer. I wanted her naked and I wanted her now.

We somehow managed to make it up to my hotel room, though only barely through the door before clothes were flying off and landing on any surface that would hold them. I thought Khloe was sexy completely dressed, but when I got her dress and undergarments free of her body, I let out a shallow whistle. She was like a woman from a porn magazine. Perfect curves, huge, heaving breasts, and the kind of ass some celebrities paid surgeries to have. Her stomach was flat, but she had some thickness to her. There was no thigh gap, and I loved every bit of it.

"Your fucking body," I hissed at her. "I know it can handle me."

"But can yours handle me?" she retorted and it

made my dick twitch with anticipation. "I dare you to try."

That wasn't a dare I needed to receive multiple times. I rolled her over until she was on her knees, and then I laid on my back and slid myself in between those beautiful, thick thighs. Her pussy hung above my face, dripping with excitement, and I was elated for the opportunity to give it everything it was begging for. I stuck out my tongue and flicked it against her hole and then traced the opening up to her clit. I sucked it until it engorged and then flipped it around with the top of my tongue.

"Ah, fuck," she moaned.

I licked back down to her hole, and poked my tongue inside, and sucked, tasting her juices. She was my new favorite liquor. I'd take it on the rocks or straight up, as long as I could have it. I released her pussy and slid further back until her pert mounds were dangling in my face. I took her nipple into my mouth and sucked while using my hand to poke into her entrance and finger her. She wiggled her hips against my hand and let out loud moans that I was sure the people in the next hotel over could hear. I attended myself to each of her nipples, and worked my way through one, two, and eventually three fingers in her tight pussy. I opened her up as much as I could so that she was good and ready to receive my dick. Soon, she threw her head back and her hips started to shudder as she drenched my hand in her ejaculate. She cried out with pleasure as she came all over me.

She shuddered until she came down off her high, and then she slid herself backwards. "I have to have you," Khloe begged. "Please fuck me."

How could I deny such a wonderful request? I used my hand to position my cock at Khloe's entrance and then ceded control as she slowly took me in. Even for having fingered her, her pussy suctioned onto my dick, grinding against it with an impossible head. She continued to move further and further until I was completely encapsulated inside of her.

"Oh my god," she sang. Her eyes rolled back in her head.

I slapped her ass hard. "Fuck that pussy is tight."

She started to ride me slowly, picking her hips up and dropping them down. The cool air outside her pussy would touch my dick and then she'd take me back into her warmth, sending pleasure rippling across my body. I had her ass clenched in my hands and was reveling in the feeling of her fucking herself on my hard member.

"You like that dick?" I asked.

Khloe nodded. "It's so good."

I slapped her ass again. "You like fucking that dick?"

"Ah!" Khloe yelped in response to the slap. "I love fucking your big dick!"

Her pace picked up as we spoke dirty to one

another, and I realized that Khloe DuBois was a true freak. The different items on the scorecard danced through my head; with her behaving the way she was, we'd have no trouble ticking the boxes there. I held onto her tightly and rolled around, flipping her so that she was under me. I anchored her as far onto her back as she would go, getting her ass up in the air, and then I started to piledrive into her, sending my dick deep into her stomach.

"Fuck!" Khloe yelled. Her hand whipped up to my head and snatched my hair into a tight fist. In any other situation it would have hurt, but it was carnal, and it turned me on. "Fuck me with that dick."

"Fucking take it," I said to her.

I slammed into her with reckless abandon, filling the room around us with lewd squirts and squelches as our fluids mixed together. Her pussy felt like a vacuum sucking me in, and my legs started to shake.

"I'm gonna fucking cum in that pussy," I said.

"Yeah, fill me up," she said. "Fill up that fucking pussy."

I grunted and groaned and a few moments later, I was emptying into her, my dick searing with heat and oversensitivity as I thrusted myself through my orgasm. When I was done, I dropped down and rested my head against her soft bosom. Her fingers loosened against my hair and rubbed my head gently. My eyelids felt ten tons heavier within a few seconds, and I only just barely managed to pull myself out and roll Khloe back over so that it was she resting on top of me. I opened my mouth to say something to her, but the sound of her rhythmic breathing found me first. Part of me wanted to be proud of the fact that she fell asleep instantly, but I knew I wasn't far behind her. I reached over to the side table, clicked off the light, and a few seconds later, I was asleep as well.

14

BRETT

*M*orning was the time that I preferred to run. Being in Puerto Rico was nice and all, but I was really lacking on my running regimen, and after a restless night of thinking about Khloe, I decided the best thing I could do for my body was run. I would put in a couple of miles, eat breakfast, and then sleep the rest of the day away until the rehearsal dinner. Hopefully it would be the rest that I needed to get through the rest of the trip with Khloe's sexy ass walking around everywhere. I slipped out of my room at about 4:00am, left the resort, and helped myself to the trail that ran along the beach. Per the signposts along the way, the path was about a mile from end to end, so I ran down to one end, back down to the other, and then back to my starting point for a nice, two-hour run.

By the time I was getting back to the resort, the

sun was just starting to peek out over the horizon. The dark blue of the night was fading into a serene cyan as the gold aura of the sun set the sea of stars on fire. Soon the sun would be high in the sky and, with any luck, I'd be one of the rare people sleeping it away.

My stomach growled as I approached the breakfast buffet, and I was glad to see that they had a schedule conducive to early risers. The sweet smell of different fruits mixed with the seasonings of eggs and a variety of meats; I was elated to be able to do some real damage. I walked inside and was surprised to see that there were a few other early birds inside, but none more interesting to me than the thick, brown-haired beauty sitting at a table in the corner, staring into her cup of coffee as though it was going to tell her future. I grabbed a cup of coffee and a plate of eggs and ham and went and joined Khloe at her table.

"You're up early," I greeted.

Khloe looked up at me and to my extreme pleasure, her cheeks instantly turned a light shade of pink. "I could say the same," she responded. "Couldn't sleep?"

The normal harshness she usually addressed us all with was gone, and she seemed renewed if not a little conflicted. "Just an early riser," I fibbed. "Went out for a run and now getting some breakfast. You look like you're trying to solve world hunger over here. You okay?"

"Um," Khloe hummed. "I think I made a really big mistake last night."

"Oh?" I replied. "Do tell." Khloe parted her lips to speak, but then clasped them shut without saying a word. "Secrets, secrets, Miss DuBois," I teased, but she didn't budge. "Fine," I said. "Can I guess?"

She seemed so lost in thought that I decided I would run a little experiment. Perhaps if I could distract her mind enough, she would be candid with me about what I believed her hangup was. I reached across the table, lifted her fork and knife, and cut a piece of the syrup soaked pancake she had sitting untouched on her plate. I poked the fork into the piece and lifted it to her lips. The blush on her cheeks darkened, but she opened her lips and let me slide the piece of pancake inside. I smiled, imagining myself shoving something else in her mouth, but that plan was going to have to wait.

"Well?" I said.

Khloe jumped a little. "Oh, sorry. Sure, you can guess."

I cut another piece of her pancake and fed it to her with a grin on my face. "Did something go wrong with the wedding?" I asked.

Khloe shook her head. "No. Not yet anyway."

I continued to feed her slowly, stopping every now and again to press my thumb to the corner of her mouth and swipe some syrup away. "Something wrong with Anna?"

"No, she's doing great," Khloe responded.

Seeing as those were the only other two things I thought it might be, that just left one possibility. "Ah, then that means you finally slept with Luke." I'd just placed a bit of pancake into Khloe's mouth and she choked on it with shock as I spoke. I dapped her lips with a napkin and chuckled. "Calm down, no one is surprised. The tension between you two was bound to break at some point. Besides, if anything, we're relieved."

"Relieved?" Khloe said. "Why?"

"Isn't it obvious? We're *all* into you," I explained. "We just needed Luke to shoot his shot so that we could get it out in the open."

"I don't understand," Khloe said. "What the hell are you talking about?"

"Luke didn't tell you? He's been something of an influence on us. Thanks to his lurid desires, we started sharing women some time ago. Obviously you've been on our radar ever since you first showed up as the wedding planner. Though I gotta say, Luke's a straight up idiot for not making a move on you sooner," I said. Khloe furrowed her brow and folded her hands into her lap, looking even more conflicted than she had before. "What?" I asked.

"What's all of your connection to one another?" She asked. "What makes you so close that you would share women?"

That wasn't a bad question. It would probably come as a shock to anyone to find out that a bunch of men intentionally shared a woman. "Well, you know Kent, Luke, Mason, David, Christian, and I all play for the Hellraisers. Well, Kent is retired because of his injuries, but that's how we met him. I know it probably seems like Luke is our ringleader, and in many ways he is, but it was Kent that brought us all together."

Khloe's eyes widened. "Wait… Did Kent share too? Did Anna—?"

I cut her off before she could finish. "No, no, no. Kent's *way* too buttoned up for that shit. He doesn't even like that we do it. No, he and Anna have always been their own thing." Khloe relaxed a little and I was glad I didn't have to shatter her image of her best friend. "So, we all knew each other from the team, and then at one point Kent ran into some real financial trouble and met Bram. He saved his life. Got him out of debt, helped him build his savings, and even helped him avoid jail for tax evasion, but you didn't hear that from me, and Anna can never know."

Khloe shook her head. "Of course."

"Then a little later on, Kent got injured," I continued.

"He can't win," she said.

I laughed. "For real. He ended up getting a concussion and that's how he met Cody. He was his trauma surgeon. He took a nasty helmet-to-helmet. He brought Cody to a game as thanks and then we all went for a beer afterwards. I was surprised he was so cool. We ended up really bonding with him and Bram. Before too long, it was like we were brothers. Luke cajoled some of us into sharing a woman and that's how we realized that with our busy lives, keeping women happy individually was a bit difficult, but if we all focused on one, it'd be good. We've had several 'trial runs,' but we still haven't found *the* one. Or shall I say, we hadn't…" Khloe stared at me intently. I could tell she was deep in thought about what I just told her, and processing the role she played in all of it. She took a sip of her coffee and stared off into space for a while. Finally I poked her gently with the fork and brought her attention back to me. "So, are you going to run now knowing the truth?"

To my shock and awe, Khloe shook her head. "No, I just have a lot to think about now, don't I?"

I bobbed my head. "I suppose so." I leaned over the table and kissed her gently on the cheek. "Don't think about it too hard, though. We wouldn't dream of pressuring you into that lifestyle."

I stood up from the table, offered Khloe a light bow, and then started off back towards my room. She did have a lot to think about, and I decided to leave her to it, not just because I didn't want her to feel pressured, but because just thinking about getting to fuck her had my dick hardening at a rapid pace.

15

KHLOE

I was a ghost wandering the halls as I made my way back to my room. I couldn't believe what Brett had told me, and how it all locked into place with what Luke was saying during foreplay the night before. They really did share women and all of them got off on watching the woman they were seeing get fucked by other men. My body boiled as I thought of myself being tossed and turned by multiple groomsmen at once. I could only imagine it would be the best sex I'd ever had, an honor currently held by Luke for his recent show. The guys were sexy, that was something I hadn't denied once since I met them, and after Luke's heartfelt apology, and Brett's sweet catering to me and feeding me during breakfast, I was beginning to think there was a different side to all of them that had stayed just outside of my field of view.

I inserted my card key into the slot on the door and heard the sound of it click just before I was assaulted by the sounds of sniffling and springs creaking. I was in a room all by myself, so I had no idea who could be making the noises from inside. I rushed in and as I rounded the corner to the bedroom, I saw Anna there, jumping up and down on the bed, bawling her eyes out.

"Anna!" I screeched and she looked down at me, but kept jumping. "What the hell are you doing? What's wrong?'

Anna stopped jumping and brought herself down to sit on the edge. Her eyes were puffy and red and there were pale streaks down her cheeks where her tears had washed away her makeup, lined by black from where her mascara had run.

"This is a mistake," she whimpered. "I'm making a huge, *huge* mistake."

"What?" I said. I walked over and knelt down in front of her. "What are you talking about?"

"Khloe, I can't do this. I can't get *married*. I can't be someone's wife. What was I thinking? Do you have any idea what it means to be a wife? Like a *wife* wife? I'm going to have to cook and clean and push babies out of my vagina!" Anna started to breathe faster and faster, and within a few seconds I could see she was hyperventilating.

I bolted out of the room and grabbed the paper bag that contained some condoms I decided to buy from the gift stop, and ran back into the room. I handed the bag to Anna, pushing it against her mouth.

"Anna," I started calmly. "You have to calm down. Breathe into the bag. Listen to my voice and breathe in," the bag crinkled as Anna breathed in, "and breathe out," the bag puffed out as Anna blew air into it. "In… and out." Anna's breathing started to return to normal, although her face was still flushed and red. "Good job. Just continue to breathe and let me talk, okay?" Anna nodded with the bag still crunching as she breathed into it. "You love Kent, more than anything in the world. You talk about it nonstop, it's so annoying." Anna giggled and pulled the bag away from her face, sniffling in as a few fresh tears streaked down her face. "I remember when you two first started dating, I'd never seen you that happy. Now you guys are getting married, and I've never seen you *this* happy."

Anna nodded. "Yeah."

"And you don't cook or clean," I said.

Anna shook her head. "I don't."

"And Kent knows that about you and proposed to you anyway!" I said.

"He did!" Anna said, sending even more tears sliding down her cheeks.

"It's because as much as you love him, he loves you," I finished and Anna's grin grew.

"He does love me. So much," she said. "I do want to have cute babies with him."

"And you will, and I will be their aunt who spoils

them and sugars them up and sends them home," I joked.

Anna wrapped her arms around me in a tight hug. I hugged her back and it filled my cup to over-flowing. I remembered why I became a wedding planner, because I loved seeing true love first hand, and I loved seeing people happy, most of all my best friend. I used my thumbs to wipe the tears off of Anna's face and then grabbed my makeup bag and handed it to her.

"Now go fix yourself, you look ridiculous." I winked and Anna gave me a kiss on the forehead and then stood up and disappeared into the bathroom.

As I waited, I realized that I'd become a wedding planner because I loved seeing true love first hand, but I'd never experienced it for myself. I'd never had someone love me the way Kent did Anna. I'd always wondered what it was like. When I thought about the situation with the guys, it made me wonder if there was any room in an arrangement like that for true love and happiness, or was it bound to crash and burn?

I saw Anna off to relax at the Spa and clear her mind from the breakdown she'd had and then I decided to head down to the beach. I hadn't really gotten to enjoy it the first time around because I was so stressed about Luke and the other grooms-men, but now that the situation with them was totally different, I could actually kick back and enjoy the wind and the water. I didn't put on my bathing suit, because I had no intentions of getting back in the water, but I grabbed a book to read and enjoy under one of the provided beach umbrellas.

I was just settling into my book when someone came and sat on the edge of my lounge chair. I looked up and Bram was sitting there smiling back at me. His looks were understated. The kind that made you think from a distance that he was just a plain, attractive enough guy, but the closer he got to you, the more you could see his cut jaw and mysterious, gray eyes. He was actually quite beautiful.

"Enjoying a book by the water?" he greeted.

"I am," I responded. "Managed to pull away from your buddies?"

He chuckled. "You're not the only one who enjoys some quiet time every now and again."

I marked my place in my book and set it aside. I wondered if Brett was really on the mark when he said that all the guys wanted me. Inquiring minds want to know; is Bram the accountant mixed up in all this sharing business as well?

"What's your relationship with all these guys? You don't seem like them," I asked.

Bram seemed slightly taken aback, but also intrigued. There was a twinkle in his eyes that made it very clear that he was attracted to me as well. His gaze scanned my form meticulously, as though he was trying to memorize it. I took his body in as well. It was clean, but ripped. Even through his t-shirt, his biceps bulged out of the sides, and his calves were defined and sharp. I couldn't help but think that he'd have no problem holding me up. He could probably do all kinds of stuff with me.

"Kent hired me to drag him from the brink of financial ruin," Bram started. "He's a smart guy, but he's not good with money. Thank god Anna is. The first thing I'm doing once those two are legal is getting all of his assets transferred into his name."

"Not a bad idea," I said, knowing Anna had a degree in Economics and was stellar with numbers and money.

"He was so convinced that I was going to be this stuffy guy, that when he realized I wasn't he wouldn't let it go. Apparently he bragged to all of his friends that he'd met 'the only cool accountant' and when they didn't believe me, he made me go out with them to prove it," Bram continued. "I actually got along with them really well, we had a lot in common, so they kept me. When they discovered that my romantic life was basically me hiring prostitutes whenever I had the chance, they decided to introduce me to their concept of sharing women for mutual pleasure. I loved it."

I continued to exchange stories with Bram over lunch and ended up enjoying his company much more than I thought I would. Surprisingly, he was something of a romantic, and told me all about how he would enjoy falling deeply in love some day, the same thing I'd just been reflecting on earlier that morning. He told me that he wasn't an easily trusting guy, so it had been hard for him to fall in love at all. He hoped that someday he would form a close enough bond with someone that he would actually feel comfortable letting his guard down and being open to love. In that instant I oddly hoped that I might be that person, and the perk to his smile told me that he hoped so too.

"So, did you just hate us all as subsets of Luke?" he asked after a while.

"Of course not," I responded even though it was an out and out lie. "I mean… Not entirely."

Bram laughed. "If not for Luke, would you have disliked me?"

I thought about it for a second even though I knew the answer. "Honestly, no. You two were so close that I thought you probably shared his attitude towards me."

"Well, I do," Bram admitted. "It's just not as sinister as you thought at first."

"Right," I replied. "I was wrong about Luke, so I guess that means that I was probably wrong about all of you."

In an instant, Bram was across the table and had his lips on mine. As he parted ways from me, he offered me a warm, sincere grin. "Maybe that means that you need to give all of us a try."

I nodded back at him. "Yeah. Maybe."

16

CODY

THE REHEARSAL DINNER

I glanced at myself in one of the floor-length mirrors in the hallway outside the rehearsal dinner space. It wasn't wedding time just yet, but I still dressed up for the occasion. I was in a pressed, navy blue suit with a light gray shirt and pocket square. I had my dark hair slicked back and had my light goatee shaved down and clean for the wedding. I pressed my jacket down, making sure I looked as good as I could, and then I entered the hall.

There weren't many people in Puerto Rico for Kent and Anna's wedding, by design. They wanted it to be small and understated, so it was just close friends and immediate family. Only a handful of the guests for the wedding weren't at the rehearsal dinner, which was just made up of Kent and Anna's parents, Kent's grandmother, Khloe, and us groomsmen. I walked in and noticed that Luke was on one side of the room murmuring to himself, probably practicing his best-man speech, and another scan revealed Khloe was clear on the other side of the room from him. There was a light hue to her face, and her eyes were darting everywhere but at him. She looked nervous, but not the 'I hate these guys' way she was typically acting, more like she was trying to hide a true nature.

On occasion, I would catch Luke glancing over at Khloe and a warm smile would cross his face. He would lock eyes with Khloe for a moment and then she would look away, but more in a coy way than frustrated. As the dinner proceeded, I noticed that a couple of the other guys, Brett and Bram, were making eyes at Khloe too. When her gaze would land on them, they would wink or smile at her, and she seemed receptive to it. She didn't seem as shy about them as she did about Luke, but things had definitely changed.

Son of a bitch, she slept with Luke. She slept with Luke and Brett and Bram know. Luke had earned 'The First One' fair and square, but we swore we would wait until after the wedding. My blood boiled, but in both a good and bad way. If Luke had broken the rules, the rest of us could as well… right? Brett and Bram were probably already planning their ways to rack up some points.

Once the dinner was over, Khloe immediately slipped out of the hall. I glanced around at the rest of the guys and when I was confident no eyes were on her or me, I followed after her. I noticed her some distance down the hallway, leaning against the wall and fanning her face. I approached her with a grin on my face, zeroing in on her like a shark to bloody waters.

"You bolted out of there like the police were looking for you," I said.

Khloe looked up at me and then rolled her eyes. "Leave me alone."

Ouch. Things seemed better with Luke, Brett, and Bram, but evidently that had not yet passed to me. "Well that's not very nice."

"I just wanted to get some air," she said.

I looked around and then back at her. "You do realize we're still inside, right?"

Khloe scoffed. "I didn't realize that, thank you, now go away."

I stepped even closer to her until I could put a hand against the wall on one side of her head. "I will not. At least not until you tell me how things went with Luke." Khloe opened her mouth to speak, but I cut her off. "No, he didn't tell me, I'm a doctor, I know the signs of sex." I used a finger to flick a piece of her hair aside. "Besides, there's a hickey on your neck." Khloe's hand flew to a spot on her neck and I let out a loud laugh. "There's no hickey, but you confirmed my suspicions, so thank you for being utterly predictable."

Khloe's eyes narrowed at me and she looked as though she was ready to chop my head off. "Why do you always do that? Why do you have to look down on me and make me feel stupid and insignificant?"

I recoiled a bit. I had no idea she felt that way. I had just assumed that we were all guilty by association with Luke, it was a shock to find out there was an actual reason she disliked me. "I didn't know I was doing that."

"All the time. I get you're a doctor and super smart, but I'm smart too, and there's no shame in an atypical career path. Just because I'm a wedding planner doesn't mean my job is any less important than yours," she spat at me.

I blinked a few times and then bowed my head. "N-no, I would never suggest that. I honestly did not realize I was making you feel that way. I'm sorry." Khloe looked up at me with annoyed disbelief, but I held up my free hand and set it to her cheek. "Truly. I didn't mean to make you feel stupid or insignificant. I believe quite the opposite to be true about you. Truthfully, I just don't think I learned how to flirt with women or really impress them in any way." I looked around and then leaned in a little more. "That's why I became a doctor. It tends to impress on its own." Unless, of course, the woman was Khloe, a perpetually difficult to impress kind of woman. "I'm still stuck in the preschool, pull a girl's pigtails, stage of flirting. I'm sorry."

Khloe's expression softened a bit. "That's okay. I don't think you're the only guy in this group who thinks that's the best way to flirt."

I thought of Luke and smiled. "Maybe that's why we get along so well." I looked into her eyes. "Since I'm not good with indirect, I'll go with direct. I'm attracted to you. I have been attracted to you for a long time, but if you just want to be with Luke, I'll back off, but we all want you."

Khloe gazed into me, the expression of curiosity shackling me to her space. "Luke told me the same thing," she admitted. Her lip curled between her teeth. "Is it wrong for me to want all of you too?"

In terms of a green light, that was all I needed. I pressed Khloe against the wall and let my lips find hers. She grabbed my waist and pulled me against her, and I wasn't about to deny her any closeness. I pushed against her until my rapidly hardening dick was poking at her, and laced my tongue into her mouth. Hers danced with mine, while Khloe herself snuck a hand between us and started to massage my dick through the fabric of my pants. I grabbed onto her breasts through her dress and started to squeeze and knead them myself, loving the way I needed to take them into full fists. She was a well endowed woman, and I had every intention of glorifying her breasts as much as they deserved. I was a breast man after all; it was only right.

Khloe moaned against my lips and I smiled realizing she had sensitive breasts. I imagined getting her nipples between a set of clamps, or wrapping some rope tightly around her boobs until they were red and begging for attention. I had plans for them, and god willing, some of those plans would be acted on before we left Puerto Rico. I pushed my knee forward, and Khloe didn't hesitate. She started to rub herself against my leg, and I felt relieved that I had gone with black for the night.

"Damn!" Khloe and I looked over and David had stumbled his way out of the party and happened upon us. "Looks like the real fun is out here. You keeping her all to yourself Cody, or could you two use a spare set of hands?"

I pulled myself back from Khloe and stepped to the side. I pinned her hands above her head and she didn't argue as David moved forward, clawed his hands up her legs and slid her thong off. He brought it to his nose and took a huge inhale and then he shoved them into his pocket. He dropped down to his knees in front of her, lifted one of her legs over his shoulder, and then his head disappeared beneath the skirt of her dress. A moment later Khloe let out a loud yelp.

"Shh," I said. "Someone will hear you."

I closed in on her and kissed her again, swallowing her moans as they left her mouth in a steady stream. I popped the top of her strapless dress down and started again at playing with her tits. I took her nipples between my fingers and pinched them, eliciting even louder moans from Khloe. She'd be a good bondage partner one day.

She melted apart in our hands as David and I worked together to pleasure her inside and out.

MASON

THE WEDDING

I was doing my best to appear really excited that someone else was getting married. I was happy for Kent, but a wedding was a wedding. There was one thing that helped. Khloe looked stunning in her peach colored, strapless dress with a ruffled skirt that stopped just above her knees. Her hair was curled half up/half down and she looked good enough to eat. All I could think about was that the wedding was nearly beyond us, which meant we could officially start making our bids for points once Luke made the first move. I expected everyone else to be in the same mode, but Luke and a few of the other guys seemed oddly at ease. In fact, the more I looked around, nearly all of them were at ease. Maybe it was just knowing it was almost over?

When it was finally time for the wedding, we all paired off. Because Anna only had one bridesmaid,

Khloe, the guys were set to walk down the aisle in pairs, with Luke and Khloe leading the way as the Best Man and Maid-of-Honor. Luke was a lucky son-of-a-bitch to get to walk with her, but I was expecting Khloe to be in low-spirits that she had to be anywhere near him at all. To my shock, however, she looped her arm through his with ease, and even had a bright smile on her face.

What the fuck was going on?

I looked over at Christian, and he seemed par for the course, but all the rest of the guys were behaving as if they'd just won the lottery. We got in line to prepare to walk down the aisle, and Christian was paired up with me.

"Hey," I whispered to him. "Are you seeing anything weird? Khloe doesn't seem as full of contempt as normal and some of the other guys are on cloud nine."

Christian shook his head. "I think it's just the wedding vibe," he said. "Khloe's probably so happy she pulled it off without Luke fucking it up, that she's actually being pleasant to him."

"Hm," I responded. It didn't seem right. Luke and Khloe weren't acting at all towards one another as they normally would. Something was up.

I had to put my suspicions aside as the wedding got underway. The ceremony was beautiful. Kent stood before a marshmallow white arch intertwined with vines and a pink and white calla lilies, with the magnificent Puerto Rican sunset as his backdrop. A pink runner led the way to the arch, and Kent and Anna's family and closest friends sat amongst a couple of dozen chairs on either side of the runner. Anna's cousin initiated the ceremony by playing live violin, and then Luke and Khloe were off down the aisle. After they went, Cody and Bram went, and they actually linked arms to be a little cheeky, and then David and Brett went after them. Finally, it was up to Christian and I, the last ones to walk the aisle before the bride.

As I walked I kept an eye on the rest of the guys and I could see them all eyeing Khloe like a hot and fresh entree that had just been delivered to their table, and what's more, Khloe had a deep red blush to her face, and kept grinning back in their direction. Had I been had? Did these bastards go behind my back and take Khloe for themselves?

Christian and I took our spots behind Kent, and then the violin changed to the traditional wedding march, and Anna appeared from behind a curtain, arm in arm with her dad. Kent took a small breath when she appeared and I could tell he was biting back tears. I was a bit jealous. I wanted to feel the kind of love that brings a person to tears. I wondered if I ever would. I couldn't help but smile broadly as Anna and Kent exchanged their vows, said their I dos, and shared their first kiss as a couple. I was happy for my friend, and I truly hoped that he had a full life of love and happiness in front of him with his new bride.

We transitioned to the enclosed tent that was the space for the reception, and once dinner had been had, I was ready to get to the bottom of everyone's random bliss. As far as I knew, Kent and Anna were the only ones who had gotten married, so I was gonna need someone to explain to me why everyone else was wearing a shit-eating grin. As soon as I noticed Cody break away from the pack and head for the bar, I followed after him.

"Hey there, Cody," I greeted.

Cody turned towards me, smiling from ear to ear. "What's up, man? Beautiful wedding, huh?"

"Whatever," I spat. "Why are you so happy?"

Cody recoiled a bit. "What?"

"Don't 'what' me. Cut the shit. Did you fuck Khloe?" I asked.

Cody's grin grew. "I didn't get that far. I had a taste though. David joined me."

My jaw dropped. "What the fuck? Weren't we supposed to wait until after the wedding? Did you jump Luke's first time to get sneaky points?"

"First of all, Luke already fucked her. You actually thought he was going to wait until after the wedding? He's not that strong." Cody took his drink from the bartender and I flagged the bartender down to get me one too. "Second of all," Cody continued, "this isn't really about the points."

"What? Of course it's about the points. That's the whole plan we made." The bartender dropped my drink and Cody and I found an unused table to sit down at. "What do you mean it's not about the points?"

"Have you actually talked to Khloe?" Cody asked. "She's pretty astounding."

I'd had the passing conversation with her, but on the whole she avoided me. Apart from our isolated incident in the grocery store, I couldn't have an extended conversation with Khloe even if I wanted to.

"So what are you saying? You like her or something?"

Cody tilted his head and stared off into space. "I could see being with her." He looked back at me. "And if you ask me, Luke's head over heels. He probably has been since high school. He was just an idiot who felt like he had to be with the head cheerleader because he was the head football player."

"That makes sense, but how do the other guys feel? Christian didn't sound like he knew," I said.

Cody nodded over his head. "David was in charge of telling him." I looked over Cody's shoulder back towards the table of groomsmen and Christian's jaw was on the table. He must have just had the news broken to him as well.

"Well fuck!" I hissed. "How could you all leave me out of all the fun? The fucking accountant gets some before me?"

"Bram?" Cody said. "I don't think he's actually gotten any yet. I could be wrong though. No one's really keeping score." That let me know that the guys felt differently about this one. In the past, we'd meticulously kept score; now suddenly Cody's saying it's not about the points, and Bram's looking like he won the lottery just because he *knows*? I must have missed something for sure. "Look, just calm down. Get through the wedding, and then we're all gonna meet up for a late night drink at the bar, Khloe included."

"Oh, I'm fucking there." I picked up my drink and stomped away from Cody. "Cheating assholes." I heard Cody snicker as I walked away.

The rest of the wedding passed at a snail's pace. I was hoping to corner Khloe at some point and see if I could get a taste of what Cody was talking about, but she was in full 'wedding planner' mode. Tending to Anna and Kent, chatting up guests, and making sure that everything went off without a hitch. She wasn't alone for a second the entire reception, and it wasn't until the wedding was over that I was able to get her alone. She left the reception right away after checking out with the tentist, and then made her way directly for the lounge. The rest of the guys were lollygagging getting out, so I took the opportunity to follow after Khloe. As she got into the lounge, I walked in after her and tapped her gently on the shoulder.

She turned around and offered me a warm smile. "Oh, hey Old Man."

I loved hearing her use my nickname. When the other guys used it, it annoyed me and even felt kind of demeaning, but when Khloe used it, it turned me on. "Hey there, young lady." Khloe wrinkled her nose, it looked adorable, but she seemed annoyed. "What's wrong? Second guessing being passed around?"

Her eyes widened. "What?"

"I know that you slept with Luke, and let Cody and David have a taste too. We have a history of sharing women, so are you officially flipping the sign to 'open?'"

Khloe scoffed. "You're a bastard. Are you trying to sabotage your friends? No wonder I didn't like you." She started to push past me, but I held out my arm to stop her. "Let me go."

"Is that why you hate me? Because you think I'm a bastard and a bad friend?" I asked.

"I hate you because everything is always a game to you when it comes to me. You treat me like a little girl and every thing that has anything to do with me, you don't take it seriously," Khloe explained with fury in her voice. "I don't need to sit here and be demeaned by you, so I'll go."

I put my arm out and stopped Khloe again. All the women I'd dealt with in the past just sort of let me do what I want, but Khloe was feisty. She stood up for herself, I liked it. "Whoa, whoa, whoa." Khloe glared at me and I took my arms off of her. "Just, I'm sorry, okay? I'm sorry. I didn't mean to come off that way. I'm so used to being the 'old man' of the group, that I treat everyone like some kid younger than me. Plus, my first wife left me because I never take anything seriously, so…"

"You're probably not a total ass," Khloe said. "You just need to communicate better."

"Yeah, communicating isn't my strong suit," I said with a chuckle. "Maybe the right girl could set me straight though."

I was beginning to see what Cody was talking about. Khloe was like a vortex. Just being near her can get you sucked in. She made me want to figure out how to be a better man. If I was making her feel demeaned and like a child, I was mad at myself for it. I only wanted to give her good emotions.

"I'm not in the business of teaching grown ass men how to be grown ass men," Khloe spat, and it shot straight to my dick. All the sentimental stuff aside, Khloe was hot as hell. "But if you're willing to try and figure it out for yourself, I can exercise more patience with you."

I smiled. "That's all I can ask of you." I took a step forward and put a hand on the side of her neck. "Can you forgive me?"

Khloe made an expression like she was still pissed, but then broke suddenly into a smile. "I suppose so."

I leaned down and pressed my lips against hers. She leaned into me and the sweetness of her coiled around me and made me never want to let go. In an instant I realized I was in trouble; that we all were. A sharp whistle split the air in half and I pulled away on reflex and looked over my shoulder. Luke was standing there with his hands in his pockets and the rest of the groomsmen behind him.

"Looks like you got started without us." He took a step forward. "She'll tell you flat out I'm her favorite, right?" He winked at her.

Khloe scoffed and rolled her eyes. "I'm not standing here while you measure dicks." She parted us like the red sea and made her way back towards the entrance of the lounge. "I'm tired, so I'm going to my room."

"Can I come with you?" Christian called after her.

Khloe looked back over her shoulder as she was walking away, laughed, and gave a little wink, and then disappeared from sight.

We were definitely in trouble. That girl already had us wrapped around her finger, and the worst part about it was, she knew it.

18

CHRISTIAN

I was beginning to wonder how long we were going to pretend Khloe was just some woman we were playing pool and sharing drinks with, and get to what we all knew we wanted. It was easy for Luke, Christian, and David, they'd already had a piece, but the rest of us were starving.

"Christian," Khloe's voice interrupted my thoughts. "Your go."

I looked at her for a minute. Her breasts spilling out over the top of her low v-cut shirt, her ass teasing me from under her tight jean shorts, her navel just barely peeking out from under the fabric. She was too much of a temptation to resist anymore.

"I have a better idea."

I started shoving all of the pool balls into the closest pocket, eliciting complaints from Khloe and all the rest of the guys when the table was clear, I walked over to Khloe, placed one arm behind her back, and one under her knees, and lifted her off the floor bridal style. I set her down flat on the pool table, snatched up one of the glasses of booze from the table's edge and poured the contents across her shirt. She gasped, but the wetness revealed her breasts exactly as I hoped it would. I then pushed up the base of her shirt, poured another glass' contents into her belly button and then licked my way across her sweet flesh to the gin awaiting me. I slurped up the liquid and Khloe let out a light moan.

"I like this idea," Mason said. He stepped up to the table and did a body shot of his own, using his hand to squeeze one of Khloe's big boobs.

We took turns taking body shots off of Khloe until she was trembling and whining out for more. I lifted her off the table and pulled her close to me and then I set my lips on hers and started to kiss her. Luke closed in on her from behind and started to rub her ass while kissing the back of her neck. Khloe linked her arms behind my neck and leaned into the feeling of Luke and I each kissing and teasing her skin.

Luke lifted his head to Khloe's ears. "Are you sure you want to do this with all of us?"

Khloe nodded. "More than you know. Merry Christmas to me."

Luke chuckled and locked eyes with me, and we knew it was showtime. I looked over one shoulder at David and he walked over to where we were standing, and then looked over my other shoulder at Mason, Cody, Brett, and Bram and they nodded. It was a silent moment of understanding between all of us. Luke, David, and I were up to bat first and then the others would get their turn. We took Khloe to the elevator to head up to David and I's room. Even on the journey up to the room, we couldn't keep our hands off of her. When the elevator doors closed, Luke latched onto Khloe's lips, I started to squeeze and massage her breasts, and David reached down to rub her awaiting pussy. Khloe mewled with pleasure as we worked her from all angles, and when the elevator doors opened on our floor, it was difficult to get her to calm down enough to get to the room.

"We're all going to fuck you," Luke growled to Khloe, pushing her down onto the hotel bed. He settled down over her and pulled her t-shirt over her head and then pulled her jeans down off of her legs. She was wearing a sexy, burgundy lace bra and thong. She was staring at Luke with nothing but lust in her eyes, and it was clear she was ready to be handled by all of us.

Luke started to act as if he was going to pull her underwear off, but I grabbed his shoulder to stop him. "Leave those on."

Luke backed out of my way as I crawled up onto the bed and released myself from my pants. I rubbed Khloe's cheek and turned her face towards me and she eagerly took me into her mouth. She hummed as she wrapped her mouth around my cock and I let out my own moan as her hot, wet throat sucked me in. Luke pushed aside the fabric of her thong and began to rub her clit.

"That's good, baby," he praised. "Suck him off while I prepare your ass for David."

Khloe looked down at Luke as best she could with my dick in her mouth and nodded. Luke then set to work fingering her pussy to keep her pleasured, while he worked a pair of lubed fingers in and out of her ass. Every single time he dove into both holes, her throat tightened around me making me weak in the knees.

Finally, Khloe popped off of my cock and looked down at Luke. "I can't wait anymore." Her eyes turned to David. "Please fuck both my holes."

"Shit," David huffed, taking his pants off and making his way over. "We got us a freak."

I repositioned so that I was standing at the head of the bed, and Khloe was on all fours. Luke slid up under her and started sucking at her breasts through the lace of her bra, while David positioned himself behind her. I watched as Luke and David each lined up to their respective holes and then pushed their way inside. Khloe had my dick in her hands, but stopped moving as they pushed in. Her face was strained with pain and pleasure; she loved being totally filled up by our three dicks.

"Relax," I said, rubbing her head.

I guided her mouth back to my cock and then we set to fucking all of her holes, and Khloe was insatiable. She turned herself into a regular sex machine, pushing herself forward against my dick, and then backwards against Luke and David in a rhythmic rotation. David slapped her ass and her tongue squeezed around my dick. I grabbed the back of Khloe's head and pushed my cock all the way down her waiting throat. She gagged on me, but didn't back off. She squelched and sucked until my dick was as far back as it could go and then she held it there in her impossible heat. Luke slammed up into her and her body started gyrating; shaking as she came.

"Fuck," David said, getting himself totally buried in her ass. "I'm gonna come."

I nodded. "Me too."

"On my face." Khloe pulled away from my dick and started to stroke it at a rapid pace with her hands. "Blow your load all over my face."

Shit. She sounded unbelievable talking to me like that. With her hands wrapped around me, her naughty words, and the sight of my friends plowing both her holes in front of me, my dick tightened and then I started to spurt out, splashing my seed all over her face.

"I'm gonna come," she warned. Having her face come on must have been a turn on for her, and David rammed into her and pulled another loud, powerful orgasm out of her.

Luke groaned in response to Khloe slamming down against his dick to ride herself through her orgasm, and David slapped her ass and pushed himself all the way into her. They both grunted as they released inside of her with Khloe moaning through an extended orgasm. David pulled out and Luke sat trying to recover, but to my shock, Khloe climbed off of the bed, and situated herself in one of the lounge chairs. She parted the lips of her pussy while keeping her eyes on me.

"Your turn," she said.

My dick was down for the count after her blow job, but I wasn't about to deny her. I stroked it to get it back up to its full hard length, and then I took my turn in Khloe's pussy, banging her in the chair while Luke and David watched. I didn't have much left in me after she was done with me, but when I was finally pulling out to come all over her stomach, I had to tap out. Fortunately, her head was laid back against the back of the chair and her eyes were drifting closed. I carried her over to the bed and set her in between Luke and David. They snuggled around her and within a few seconds, they were all snoozing away.

I went into the bathroom and took a long, hot shower. I lost track of how long I was inside, but eventually the sounds of Khloe moaning found my ears. I turned the water off and walked out of the bathroom and saw her spit roasted on the bed between Mason and Brett. Mason had his dick shoved down her throat, and Brett had his dick in her pussy and a bright, pink dildo vibrating inside her ass. She was screaming with pleasure, even with her mouth stuffed up by Mason. I wanted to join in, but I would need longer to recover than our apparent energizer bunny. I was going to head into the other room to try and get some sleep when I noticed Luke sitting on the couch watching Mason, Brett, and Khloe with a confused look on his face.

Khloe looked over at him and he let out a light gasp.

"You good?" I asked.

Luke stood up from the couch. "I gotta go." He raced past me and out of the hotel room without another word.

19

CODY

was thrilled when I finally got the text that it was my turn to take our new lover for a spin. I smacked Bram awake and told him we were up and he was out of bed quicker than I'd ever seen the man move in his life. I dipped into my room briefly to grab the emergency items I'd purchased after the rehearsal dinner, and we made our way to Christian and David's room, the apparent epicenter of Khloe's orgy.

When we got to the door, I motioned for Bram to stay outside for a second and then I walked in. When I rounded the corner, and she was laying on the bed, stark naked, with Mason and Brett passed out on either side of her. When I walked in, her face lit up. "Oh good," she said with a smile. "I wrung these two out, but I'm not done yet."

She was like an evil witch in disguise from a fantasy movie. She fooled us with her faux-innocence and pretending like we were the big, bad groomsmen treating the poor innocent princess badly. In reality, she was a queen atop her throne, sifting her way through her concubines until she was fully satisfied, and I got the sense that level of satisfaction would be hard to reach. I had something lined up for her though, something bound to knock the wind out of her sails.

I reached out for her hand, which she took, and I pulled her off the bed. I led her to the doorway to the bedroom, and stood her in the frame. I reached into my bag and pulled out a coiled rope. I wrapped it around her wrists a few times and then secured it to the top of the door frame using an included set of clasps. I took matching sets and tied each of her ankles to the door frame as well so that she was fastened inside the frame, with her limbs totally restrained. I then reached into my bag and pulled out a blindfold and tied it around her eyes. I stepped back and admired the view of her stretched out, bare body just waiting for me to have my way with it.

I beckoned Bram inside, with my fingers placed to my lips to keep him quiet. He sat down in a chair facing the doorway and pulled out his dick and began to stroke. I made my way back behind Khloe and without any warning, smacked her ass. She jumped and let out a loud yelp. I did it again and she threw her head back.

"Yes!" she cried.

So I smacked her ass again. I alternated cheeks until each of them had taken a fair amount of abuse, then I pulled my dick free and started to slap it against her pussy. She was soaking wet and dripping all over. I didn't enter her yet though. I slid my dick back and forth across her wet lips until she was trembling.

"Stop teasing," she whimpered. "I want you to fuck me."

She was pulling at her restraints, attempting to increase the friction herself, but I had her pulled tight to the frame. She had no control at all. I kept sawing my dick along her pussy and poking my head at her clit. She cried out each time I nudged her sensitive spot, but whenever it seemed like she was close to cumming, I pulled away. She whined and writhed against the ropes, stick her ass back and coaxing me to fuck her. She was a naughty girl, and if she wanted my dick that badly, who was I to deny her? We'd get into a complete sensory deprivation, edging and releasing session at some point, but I was ready to be inside her just as much as she was ready to have me inside, so I pressed my dick against her hole and slammed into her all in one, hard thrust.

"Fuck!" Khloe yelled. "Fuck me!"

I dug my fingers into the flesh of Khloe's thighs and rammed in and out of her. Each time my balls slapped against the skin of her pussy, the clenched tighter inside and my dick felt like it was going to explode.

"Fuck, you feel so good," I huffed at her.

"I love your dick," Khloe responded, throwing her ass back as best she could. I slapped each cheek again as I fucked her, eliciting even louder cries of pleasure.

Finally, I reached up into her hair and pulled the blindfold from her eyes. She noticed that Bram was sitting there watching her, and the tightness of her pussy doubled.

"I think she could use some sweetness," I said to Bram.

Bram stood up and went to my bag and reached in and pulled out a can of whipped cream. He sprayed some of the white substance onto her breasts and down her stomach and then went to work enjoying licking it off. Khloe moaned as his tongue slurped over her breasts, cleaning off all of the whipped cream.

"Only whipped cream?" Khloe asked.

Bram smiled and reached into the bag and pulled out a bottle of chocolate syrup. "What's a sundae without fudge?"

I untied her from the door frame, and we moved over to the couch. I pulled out of Khloe and Bram bent her over the back of it. I went and stood in front of her, perching my dick at her mouth, and Bram reached over her, and squirted a bunch of the chocolate onto my dick. Khloe licked her lips and then took my dick into her hands and started to lap up the chocolate like a dog to peanut butter. Bram squeezed some more of the chocolate over Khloe's ass and pussy and then crouched down and began to lick it up. Khloe moaned around my dick as Bram serviced her below. She licked all around my dick until every ounce of it was cleaned up, and then she turned to just giving me a blow job, the best one I'd ever had. She bobbed her head up and down on my rock hard cock until I was ramming against the back of her throat. I let a moan escape my lips as the combination of being inside Khloe and then having her suck me off, threatened to pull me over the edge.

Bram finished licking the chocolate off of Khloe's intimate parts and stood up to line himself up behind her. "Should I fuck your ass?" he said.

Khloe nodded. "Please fuck my ass."

Bram didn't hesitate. He plunged himself into her ass, rubbing his hands all over her asscheeks, which were still bright red from my earlier torment. He took fistfuls of her flesh and dove as deep as he could, slamming so hard against her that I could barely hear her moans over the slaps of his skin against hers. She started to suck me to the pace of his thrusts, and I couldn't even get a warning out. The base of my stomach and edge of my thighs tingled, and I tracked my orgasm as it shot through my dick and out into Khloe's mouth in white ribbons. She sucked as she drank every bit of my cum, turning her attention then to tossing her ass backwards to meet Bram's thrusts.

"I'm gonna fucking cum on this ass," Bram hissed.

Khloe nodded. She looked back over her shoulder at Bram with her eyes still watering from choking on my cock. "Come all over my ass."

Bram drove himself into her a final few times and then grunted loudly. He ripped his dick from her ass just in time for his cum to splat out all over Khloe's sexy, round ass. We all sat there breathing in the wake of our orgasms, until Khloe finally crawled over the back of the couch and laid on it outright. I climbed in behind her and spooned her from behind, and Bram sat on the edge of the couch and rubbed her feet. If anything happened after that, it was nothing more than a blur to me. I caressed Khloe's skin gently until I eventually faded from consciousness.

My heart was still racing as I got back to my room. In the instant that I locked eyes with Khloe, something clicked in me, and I knew I wasn't just playing around with lust anymore. Just that glance she gave me rocked me to my core and proved to me in an instant that I was far past a line I didn't remember crossing. My skin was clammy and sweat was falling down my head. I was… in love. I couldn't deny it. When did it stop just being about getting Khloe in bed? When did I start to think of her as much more than that? The truth of the matter was, I had never been in love before. Maybe that was the problem. I didn't know how to identify the feelings when they happened, so I didn't realize when they snuck up on me with a bat covered in nails.

"Fuck," I hissed aloud to myself. I was in love.

I pulled off my suit coat jacket and tossed it to

the side, and I heard the small clack of something hitting the ground. I walked over and noticed that a piece of paper had dropped out of my pocket. I picked it up and unfolded it and chuckled. It was the totally unused scorecard. Not once since I first slept with Khloe had any of us worried about the 'points' we were racking up. No one had mentioned any of the areas they got to first and no one really seemed concerned with winning the competition. Maybe we would still take a trip out of the country, maybe we would take Khloe with us, but it wouldn't be because we won some stupid contest, it would be because we wanted to go and had an amazing woman that we wanted to spoil.

I walked over to the trash can, and started to drop the paper inside, when I got a bit curious. It would be kind of funny to tease the guys if I had gotten the most points, even if they don't matter anymore. I walked back over to the hotel desk, grabbed a pen, and started to fill in the scorecard. I wrote Khloe's name on top, and then started to tally the points. I, of course, got the big 75 points for being Khloe's first, so I filled those in under my name, and then I knew Cody and David had taken her at the rehearsal dinner, but I also got a blowjob in the lounge, so all three of us got 30 points for sex in public. Christian, the sneaky bastard, started off the body shots, so he technically got the first 20 points for food/drinks, but Bram went to her hotel room prepped with chocolate and whipped cream, so he got 20 points too.

Cody ventured into light bondage, which was worth a whopping 40 points, and technically Bram was in on that too, so the dumb accountant and doctor were knocking at my door for the most points, but fortunately I still had a few more and there was more to tally. Christian, David, and I did a little bit of foreplay in the elevator, so we would get the extra 10 points for that, and David was also the first one to take her anally, the other big one on the card for 50 points, and then I got a residual 20 points for also doing her anally, as did Mason. Brett introduced toys as well, so he got 30 points for that.

In the end David had 90 points, Cody had 70, Bram had 60, Christian had 30, Brett also had 30, and Mason, the poor guy, only had 20. I grinned with pride as I looked at my total. I demolished them with an impressive 135 points. I laid the scorecard out on the desk and took a picture with my camera phone. We were probably all past caring about getting points with Khloe, we actually had feelings for her, but a little light jabbing never hurt anyone, especially when I was technically the victor.

A knock at the door seized my attention. I slipped my phone into my pocket and walked over to the door and peeked through the peephole. My heart started to race as I laid eyes on Khloe, dressed in a simple jeans and t-shirt ensemble, with her hair up, and cheeks still looking as though she was turned up from her last round with Bram and Cody.

I opened the door and she smiled wide at me. "Hello," she greeted.

I wrapped an arm around her and pulled her into me, dropping my head to hers to kiss her. "Hello," I responded after taking a sweet taste of her lips. "What? Are you after the world record for most orgasms in a period of time?"

Khloe giggled and it may as well have been birds singing in a romance movie. It set me on fire. I was definitely in love with her. "No, I'm just here to get to know you better. I want to know the real Luke, not the asshole who tortured me in high school, or the sex god who gave me more orgasms in one go than I have ever had, probably combined."

I liked that title. Luke, the sex god. I put that out of my mind for the moment and bring Khloe the rest of the way inside. I wanted to get to know her more too. I wanted to know everything about the woman I loved. I led her to the couch in my suite's living room area, and then ordered some ice cream and wine from room service. When it arrived, we got comfortable under a blanket on the couch, I put on some music, and we just sat and talked. I'd never experienced just talking with a woman before. If it was possible, I was even more attracted to Khloe than I had been at first.

"So, your dad seriously kicked you out just because you decided not to go into the army?"

Khloe asked in the wake of something I'd never told anyone before.

I nodded. "My dad, my grandpa, and my great-grandpa were all military men. High ranking ones too. My dad said that it was my civic duty to serve my country, but being a military brat nearly ruined my life as a kid. I'm sure it's why I was such a dick. I didn't want that life for myself as an adult, or for my future children, so I told him I wasn't doing it. He kicked me out at 15 and I had to go and live with my aunt, his sister. She took care of me like her own though, and now I get to take care of her with the money I make playing."

"My aunt was huge in my life too," Khloe said. "My mom was a single parent to me and my brother, and it was hard on her. She couldn't afford childcare, so my aunt would take care of us because she owned her own business, a bakery. When she was at home, we'd get to hang out at home with her, and as we got older, we got to spend more time with her in the bakery. I would see all the couples come in to get their wedding cakes, and then she let me help her with my brother's wedding, and that's what inspired me to become a wedding planner."

"Wow, that's awesome," Luke said. "My aunt is a lawyer. She's a little stuffy, but she loves hard. I'm so grateful for her."

Khloe rested her head against my shoulder and carefully stroked the palm of my hand. It was so small, but somehow otherworldly intimate. I had never experienced anything like it before..

"So, now that we've gotten to know each other better, has your lust for me died out?" she asked.

I blew out a raspberry. "Are you kidding? With *this* body. If I ever stop lusting after you, assume I've been replaced by a body snatcher."

Khloe laughed, but it turned into a yawn. She'd had a long 24 hours pleasing all of us, it was only fair that she was tired. I stood up from the couch and took her into my arms and carried her into the bedroom. I laid her down on the bed and settled behind her, kissing her cheek and stroking her hair until I finally heard her snoozing softly, then I rested my head against hers and drifted off myself.

The next morning, I slipped out of bed as quietly as I could and went to go after some coffee and bagels. Now that the wedding was over, we'd be headed back for Texas soon and had a day of packing and getting ready to leave ahead of us. Khloe was going to need a little boost, and as her new love-interest, I was the perfect person to give it to her. I was almost annoyed at myself for grinning like an idiot the whole time I walked down to the cafe and back up to the room, but when I opened the door to the hotel room, my good mood was dashed in a second. I stepped into the living room and Khloe was sitting on the couch with a piece of paper in her hands. Her eyes were red and puffy and the paper was wrinkling at the edges where it was clenched in her hands. I glanced at the desk and my heart shattered. The scorecard was no longer there; Khloe was gripping it, with pain on her face.

"Khloe, I swear to god, that is not what it looks like," I started.

Khloe looked up and me and I wanted to crawl into a hole and die. I couldn't believe that I had caused her so much pain. "So this isn't a scorecard with all sorts of points that you all have been getting for doing different sexual stuff with me?"

I could hear Kent in my head telling me that the scorecard was a bad idea. If only we had listened. "Well... technically, that's what it is, but—"

Khloe stood up and stormed over to me. "I hope you had fun."

She forced the scorecard into my chest and then started off around me. I didn't have any free hands to grab her with, so she got away while I was setting the coffee and bagel bag down. I rushed out after her, but didn't make it before she was in her own room with the door shut and locked behind her. I pounded on the door despite the early hour, just trying to get her to open up.

"Khloe, please, let me explain," I begged.

Khloe opened the door and looked directly into my eyes. "There's only one thing I need to know. Was it ever part of some plan to tally points for sex with me?" I stared at her. I knew that if I told her the truth I would lose her, but I also knew that she already knew the truth and if I lied I would lose her too. I didn't know what to do. "Answer me."

"In the beginning," I admitted. "I'm so sorry."

Khloe shook her head as a few fresh tears fled down her cheeks. "Never come near me again. Tell your friends the same."

The door slammed in my face, shattering the blissful world I was just getting used to, and dealing me my very first ever heartbreak.

BRETT

It had been a long 5-hour ride home. Khloe hopped an early flight home, managed to completely avoid us up until the time she had to leave. All flight I had to sit there and imagine her exhausted and upset, and know that her final opinion of me was going to be that I was a guy who tricked women into thinking they actually liked them to score points in some stupid men's game. None of the women we had ever scored in the past had any false belief that we wanted a relationship with them. They were just in it for the sex as much as we were, they just didn't realize we were keeping score, but Khloe was different. Khloe actually meant something to us, the first woman who'd ever meant something to us, and her heart was broken thinking that we didn't care about her at all.

I couldn't believe my dumb fucking luck.

Sharing women with Luke was bound to have a downside at some point, I just didn't realize it would happen when I'd found such a perfect one. Finally a woman that I could actually see myself being with for the long haul and Luke had to go and mess everything up being an idiot. We'd gathered at his place for him to explain what happened after he'd hastily told us that Khloe 'probably hates us for good now' with no additional explanation before getting on the plane.

"Why did you even still have that list?" I hissed. "It was obvious we liked her more than that. You should have shredded it as soon as it became real!"

"I forgot I even had it! Besides, don't act like this list shit is all about me, we were all there when we made the fucking thing. You were all too stoked about it back when we made it, you're just pissed that you didn't get any fucking points!" Luke bellowed.

"Fuck you, you dick!" I yelled back. "Finally, Khloe actually starts coming around to the idea of being with us and you actually let her see the score-card? How dumb can you be?"

My skin started to sizzle with heat. That he could even suggest that I was upset for any reason other than losing Khloe made me feel like he sabotaged us on purpose. All he had to do was not let her see the damn thing, so instead he goes and leaves it out in the wide open for her to view at her leisure. What a moron. Luke continued to glare at me as though I actually had some role to play in costing us all the best woman we'd ever had, and something in me just snapped. I cocked my fist back and blasted it straight at Luke's face, making hard contact with his left cheek.

"Brett!" Cody barked. Luke lunged back at me, trying to get a lick back in to retaliate for mine, but I ducked it and pulled him into a standing choke-hold. "Guys!" I felt a few sets of hands on me, forcing Luke and I apart. I let him go and David and Mason pulled him away and held him back, while Cody and Bram held me. "It doesn't make any sense to fight," Cody continued.

"You mean to tell me that you aren't pissed as hell that you lost Khloe because of this jackass?" Christian cut in. "She hates us now, because of him."

Cody shook his head. "We *all* made that list."

"Yeah, but only one person threw it in her face," I said. "It doesn't bother you. Imagine how Khloe must feel about you right now? She thinks that she was just points to you. Everything you did, all of that work we put in to get her to see us in a different light, all she thinks now is that it was all for show. All that horrible stuff she thought about us, Luke made it true."

"She's so great, and you knew that more than anyone," Christian said, with a look of disappointment on his face. "Why would you screw that up?"

"I honestly didn't mean to," Luke said. "I forgot I had that paper."

"Did you also forget that you pulled it out and filled in all the points?" I asked, irritation thick in my voice.

Luke bowed his head, his cheek already bruising from the punch. "I should have thrown it away; I just thought it would be funny. An inside joke for us, and nothing else. She showed up at my door and I was so distracted by her being there, that I completely forgot I'd even taken it out." He looked at me and he looked like he was on the brink of tears. "I'm sorry."

I shook my head. "I don't wanna hear it. I'm out."

"Me too," Christian said.

We both grabbed our things and left the apartment without another word. I headed straight for my gym, found a punching bag, and went to town. I needed to call Khloe on my own and see if I could at least get my own name cleared, but I had to calm down first, and I definitely needed to have a better idea of what I wanted to say.

"Hey Khloe," I greeted her voicemail when I called her a few hours later. "Luke told us what happened and I just wanted you to know that I'm so sorry. I can't imagine how hurt you must feel, but you have to believe me that we made that scorecard way before we started up anything with you. Even before we thought we really had a chance. As soon as you were willing to be with us, we all couldn't get over how great it was. We all said how we really liked you and that it wasn't just a typical girl for us. Luke was supposed to destroy that thing… not that that's any excuse. Anyway, if you feel like hearing me out, give me a call. I don't plan on getting over you anytime soon."

Over the course of the next week, we all tried to reach out to Khloe, and all tried to get her to hear us out. We left her as many voicemails as we could before her voicemail box started reading as full, and then we took to sending her texts and emails; anything to get to her. It wasn't until Bram cautiously reminded us that we were bordering on harassment that we decided to lay off.

We met at a bar to mourn the death of our relationship before it had even begun, but both Christian and I struggled with Luke being there. It was his fault that everything went awry, and I just couldn't bring myself to forgive him. Every time I even thought about it, I remembered our nights with Khloe and it made my blood boil all over again. I couldn't enjoy sex like that with a different woman even if I wanted to, they may be good, but they would be no Khloe.

"There's gotta be something we can do," David said. "She likes us, right? I mean, I told her how I feel."

"We all did," Bram said. "Nothing's working."

"Wow, you seven look like the sorriest pack of wolves I've ever seen." I looked up and Kent was walking into the bar, back from his honeymoon. "Seems to me like you should have listened to your good friend Kent, but no. What do I know? I'm just the only one of us who *actually* managed to get a girl to spend more than a week with him." He took Luke's beer from in front of him and started drinking it. "Khloe's smart, beautiful, funny, has her shit together, and was willing to fuck all of you. Why wouldn't you fuck that up?"

"Dude, maybe you and Anna can have a barbecue or something?" Luke said. "Invite all of us and Anna can invite Khloe. We can all show up with a dozen roses, no, a dozen bouquets of roses. We can apologize in person and try and win her back."

"Yeah, that's not gonna work because Anna wants to murder all of you," Kent responded.

"Women stick together like that," Cody said.

"Well, that and the fact that Khloe's moving to California," Kent said.

All of us froze in place. "W-what?" Luke said.

"She's going to stay with the woman who did our flowers, her friend Cece. Anna's been trying to talk her out of it all week, but she called this morning to say that she booked a flight out tomorrow," Kent explained.

I glared over at Luke and I noticed Christian glaring too. Even the other guys at the table, though not as angry, had their eyes on Luke with disdain.

Not only had we lost Khloe in our relationship, but now she was moving out of Texas? We'd never see her again. My heart ached and I actually felt like I could cry. Never see Khloe again? I did not agree to that.

Luke stood up suddenly from the table. "I'm going after her."

"What?" Kent said.

"I have to go. I have to tell her to her face that I'm sorry. I can convince her to forgive us, I know it," Luke said.

Kent shook his head. "Dude, forget it. She's torn up right now, the last thing she wants is to see you."

"Yeah, you went after her back in Puerto Rico too, and you just made it worse," Christian said.

"I wasn't going to lie to her," Luke demanded. "I have to go."

"We can't," Mason said suddenly and all of our eyes shot to him. "We have to give her space now."

Luke's jaw dropped. "But—"

Mason grabbed Luke by the arm and pulled him back down into his chair. "They say if you love something, you have to let it go. Khloe will take the time she needs and if she feels like she can find it in her heart to forgive us, after everything we've said, then she'll come back. If she doesn't, then that's her answer and we have to respect that."

"Mason's right," Cody said. "We *all* fucked up when we agreed to diminish her to points like that. Whether Luke was the one who let her see it or not, this is our punishment. We've said all we can say, it's up to her now."

The table fell to silence as we realized that what Mason and Cody were saying was true. We had to just wait and hope that Khloe would come around. If she didn't, we'd respect that. We'd have to.

22

KHLOE

I sat in the airport waiting for my flight to California. I sent my friend Cecilia "Cece" Cassini a text to let her know I'd arrived at the airport and would see her in a few hours. She texted back almost instantly telling me that she couldn't wait to see me, but wished that I wasn't so heartbroken. I thought back a few weeks to when it was me comforting Jordan who was heartbroken from several men. When she was sitting on my couch, explaining her situation to me, all I could think to myself was, 'the signs were right in front of you, how did you not see it?' Maybe that same cruel god who'd been haunting me since I first saw Luke walk into the very first meeting of Kent's groomsmen was still determined to see to it that I was punished for a sin I didn't realize I'd committed. How cruelly ironic that it would be me sitting in the hot seat, wondering how I'd missed the signs and allowed myself to be hurt so badly. Of course those men didn't actually think of me as anything more than meat; how could they? Luke hadn't changed, he had just given over more power to his dick.

After getting back from Puerto Rico, I tried to return to normal. Jordan was still staying at my place and it was beginning to look like she'd be there for a while. Despite the fact that she had been through something similar, I couldn't bring myself to talk about it with her. I was too embarrassed. I had only let the guys in for a few days; I chalked it up to getting swept up in the moment in a different country. That's what I tried to convince Jordan of. There was nothing that happened that I couldn't put behind me. That's what I tried to convince myself, but suddenly the guys were everywhere. Even when they were just Kent's stupid grooms-men, I could avoid them when I didn't have to see them, but now that I had feelings for them, I couldn't leave my house without finding one of them. At first, I thought they were *trying* to be places that I was, but then they started calling and texting me non-stop and I realized that if any of them realized they were in the same place as me, they would have acted on it.

I saw Mason while I was shopping at the grocery store, apparently Brett and I went to the same gym, Cody was randomly at the same bistro downtown that I liked to go to, and Bram's accounting firm had a satellite office right across the street from my pilates studio. David's running routine took him around the same park where I would sit to work on nice days and Christian often brought his dog to the dog park at the park a few blocks away that I tried to flee to in order to avoid David. Worst of all, Luke was being heralded as the Hellraisers' Player of the Year. His face was plastered on every newspaper and billboard in Austin. I had to get out of town.

Anna tried hard to convince me not to leave. She told me that she would help me get over the guys, and even offered to help me find 'ten new guys if it would help,' but nothing she said could quell the way my heart broke when I laid in bed alone at night. I had to put distance between myself and Austin; between myself and these seven groomsmen who destroyed me. So I was headed to California. Despite what I'd told Anna, I hadn't actually made the decision to stay for good, but if it felt like I could start over, then I would. It didn't seem like Jordan was going home any time soon. If she needed to, she could take over my lease, get a new nanny job in Austin, and we could both start fresh in new cities.

While I was waiting, I got another message from Anna, begging me not to go to California and reprimanding me for not clearing out my voicemail so that there was space for her to leave another. I texted her back to assure her I didn't have a full voicemail to avoid her, but she didn't believe me.

What she didn't know is that my voicemail was full to bursting with voicemails from all of the guys. I hadn't checked any of them. I knew that I should just go in and delete them, but for some reason, I couldn't bring myself to do it. It felt like the last of what I had of them, and whenever I thought about clearing them out, I convinced myself that there was some stupid reason I should hold off. I navigated to my voicemail and saw the seven messages from each of the guys and my heart swelled. Each message was a minute or more. They weren't just saying 'call me.'

They deserved a listen for that, right?

I clicked on Bram's first. My studious, clean cut accountant. "Hey... babe? Is babe okay? What does it matter, you probably don't want to hear anything from me at this point. Look, I know you're upset and my voice is the last thing that you want to hear but... truth told, I had to hear your voice. I called just to hear you on your voicemail, and now I'm leaving you a message and sound like a creepy stalker. I'm sorry for everything. We never should have made that stupid list, it was just a joke. Did I actually think I was ever going to get to lick chocolate and whipped cream off of your smoking hot body? No. That's shit that I only dared dream about. Then it finally happened and we've gone and fucked it up. You didn't deserve that, and I would give anything to take it back. If nothing else, please know that I never meant to hurt you. When we talked about wanting to find true love one day, I really thought that could be possible with us. I guess I'll just put that back in my vault of dreams. Take care of yourself, beautiful girl, I'll miss you."

My heart cracked. Bram sounded so sincerely sad that I felt compelled to call him right away and tell him I forgave him, but that scorecard ran through my brain and I remembered. He did one of the things explicitly stated on the scorecard. How could I truly believe he didn't take the points seriously?

Mason's was next. "What's up, old lady?" I couldn't help but smile. "Look, I'm not much for words. You said so yourself, I have to get better at communicating. You promised that if I was willing to try and improve, that you'd be patient with me, so I'm callin' in that favor. I'm sorry that you saw that dumb scorecard. It didn't mean anything. Some stupid points on a piece of paper? You know Luke's as arrogant as they come. He was supposed to rip it up and instead he filled it out just to fuck with us. You weren't supposed to see it. Well... we never should have made it. I'm sorry you must feel so shitty, but if you come back, I promise I'll beat Luke into a fucking pulp and you can watch."

The line immediately went dead. Mason wasn't good at communicating, but I chuckled thinking about him kicking Luke's ass. I knew he'd do it if I truly asked him to.

"Khloe," Cody said at the beginning of his

message. "Um…" He let out an awkward chuckle. "What can I say? I feel like the biggest jerk around. We shouldn't have even made that scorecard. We all believed it was a pipe dream anyway, and that's the honest to god truth. Kent called us idiots to our faces for thinking it may actually happen, and for what it's worth, he also was disgusted by our making it. For what it's worth, seeing my name on that paper made me hate myself. Knowing that I was part of anything that caused you pain kills me. I hope that, even if we never meet romantically again, that someday you forgive me. Take care."

No one would guess that Cody was the confident doctor from how meek and depressed his message sounded. To think I once thought of him as the arrogant one; he sure turned that around.

Next up was Christian. I played the voicemail and was just met with singing. The words were only half legible. It was clear he was wasted. "…and I think you're great! …Panda bears!" I was laughing out loud while listening to Christian croon. "Love or something,…" My heart beat a little faster. I wished I knew what he was saying. The line went dead mid-word and I just let out a laugh. I anticipated he accidentally hung up on himself. It was pretty good.

David was the next one. "Bonjour, Bella." David spoke French fluently, something I'd learned somewhere along the way. "Look, I could tell you that I'm sorry, and that this was all just a big misunderstanding, but I'm sure you've heard that from everyone else. Instead, I want to tell you how proud I am of you for not immediately hunting each one of us down and cutting off all of our dicks. I heard some of the threats you threw at Luke, I know you're capable of it." I smiled, remembering how awful I used to be to them, even though they deserved it. "I miss having your dry wit around us. We need you, Khlo. We're not good without you. I can't say anything to convince you that we aren't the dicks that you already know we are, but if you don't come back and we don't get better, you have only yourself to blame. Miss ya, kid."

The line went dead, and I felt warm inside. Hearing the guys' apologies one after the other was softening me a bit. I was inclined to believe they were sorry, they had to know the mistake they'd made.

Brett's was the oldest, he tried first. "Hey Khloe, Luke told us what happened and I just wanted you to know that I'm so sorry. I can't imagine how hurt you must feel, but you have to believe me that we made that scorecard way before we started up anything with you. Even before we thought we really had a chance. As soon as you were willing to be with us, we all couldn't get over how great it was. We all said how we really liked you and that it wasn't just a typical girl for us. Luke was supposed to destroy that thing... not that that's any excuse.

Anyway, if you feel like hearing me out, give me a call. I don't plan on getting over you anytime soon."

I decided to skip Luke's in the line as I was scrolling through. I didn't think I could handle hearing his voice. He was the one who let me see that awful thing, and when I asked him about it, he admitted to my face that the original plan was to follow the scorecard.

"That's right," I said aloud.

Regardless of what all the guys had said, Luke had told me the truth. They made the scorecard with every intention of racking up points at my expense. They were trying to convince me that it was just a prank, but they made it to begin with. It was well drawn out, they had points designated to everything; they had done it before and they did it with me. I deleted all the voicemails except for Luke's and shoved my phone into my bag.

When I got to California, I was going to listen to that voicemail and formulate a carefully and strongly worded text to send to all of them. I was going to let them know that I was done for good and that I never wanted to hear from any of them ever again.

23

CODY

"I think we've got everything under control, Doctor." The nurse held out a slip for me to check over and sign off on and I glanced it over. I was on call at the ER all night, but I was checking out for a couple of hours to eat dinner and sleep. I signed the paper and handed it back to the nurse I was speaking with. "Thank you. You know how to get ahold of me if you need me. I'm not going off site."

The nurse nodded back at me. "Yes sir. Enjoy your dinner."

"Thanks," I murmured back.

He started to walk away from me, but then he looked back over his shoulder. "Uh, is everything okay?"

My eyes widened a bit. "What?"

"Oh, you just seem, I don't know, sadder than

usual. I mean, it isn't as if you're Tickle me Elmo or anything, but normally you're more upbeat, or at least content. Ever since you got back, you seem out of sorts."

It was weird hearing it explained that way. I guess I hadn't noticed, but losing Khloe had much more of an effect on me than I realized. "Truthfully? I'm going through a breakup right now."

The nurse frowned. "Oh, I'm sorry, that's no fun. Well, take care of yourself. Stay hydrated, don't become a hermit. I went through that last year, so I know how difficult it can be."

I nodded. "Thanks."

He gave me a final smile and then headed off. It was weird speaking about Khloe like a thing of my past. I'd only just gotten the chance to be with her, and I really thought it was going to be the real thing. I went and collected my phone and wallet and then made my way down to the hospital cafeteria. I thought of the nurse's warning to 'not become a hermit' and rolled my eyes. It wasn't holing up in my house that I needed to be concerned about, it was holing up in my job. If I was working, I wasn't thinking about Khloe, and if I wasn't thinking about Khloe, I could at least get some modicum of peace.

I should have gone out for lunch, to get out of the hospital for a bit, but I honestly didn't want to. I didn't want to do much of anything. I was just settling down to eat a sandwich and some soup when I got a call from Luke. Going through a breakup was hard, but going through the same breakup as your best friends was near impossible to deal with. I felt like I couldn't get my act together, but Luke was a complete wreck. With some of the guys not even having forgiven him yet, I was doing my best to cater to him when I could.

I answered my phone with a sigh. "Hey man."

"Hey," Luke responded. "Are you at work?"

"Yeah, I'm on call all night." I took a quick bite of my food. "What's up, you doing okay?"

"When's your next break?" he said, ignoring my question.

"I'm on break right now."

"Can I come meet up with you?"

"Oh, yeah man, of course. I'm in the cafeteria at the hospital."

"Okay. I'm at the hospital now too, so I'll be there in a second." I wanted to ask what he was already doing here, but before I could get the words out, the line clicked dead. It made me nervous. Luke was never that short.

A few minutes later, Luke entered the cafeteria, and despite the number of good looking women who worked for the hospital that locked eyes on him immediately as he walked in, he didn't seem concerned with them at all. He headed over to my table and sat down across from me.

"I'm sorry," Luke said immediately. "I'm sorry I messed this up for us."

"You don't have to keep apologizing," I said. "I

know that some of the other guys are mad at you alone, but that list was all of our mistakes. We ruined this for ourselves. All of us."

"Why can't I get over it?" Luke said. "It was only a couple of days."

"For us it was a couple of days, but for you it's been ten years," I explained. "You may not think you liked Khloe back in high school, but you've told me stories that make me think you did. You felt pressured to bully her so you did, but those times when you were watching her in the library or following her down the halls. It was because you liked her."

Luke sat contemplating this. I could see in his face that he knew I was right, but that probably didn't make things any easier. "Well, I don't know what to do anymore. Kent's still pissed that I broke his rule to begin with because Anna's all upset, and Christian and Brett won't even talk to me. Anytime I see Mason, Bram, or David, even though they're not mad at me, I can see it in their faces, I'm just a reminder of the fact that they lost Khloe. I can see that look in your face too."

I sighed. I wanted to pretend as if that wasn't true. As if I wasn't contributing anymore to Luke's frustration, but when I saw him, it did force my brain back to the memory that we lost her. I'm sure he could see that in my face. "I'm sorry."

"Don't be sorry," Luke said. "It's my fault." I opened my mouth to argue, but Luke held a hand up. "It's fine. I know the role I played in it is larger than any of the rest of you. I've made peace with that fact. That's why I'm leaving too."

I nearly spit out my food. "What?"

"I'm up for free agency," Luke explained. "I wasn't going to leave the Hellraisers, and they were planning on renewing my contract, but Miami made me an offer and I think I'm going to take it. I'm headed down there tomorrow to hear them out."

My jaw dropped. "You can't just run from the problem."

"There's no problem to run from," Luke responded. "This just *is* now. We lost Khloe. She moved to California. That's it. We've lost the woman we love."

The last word struck me like a cinder block over my head. I hadn't been willing to admit as much to myself, but it was the truth. From the moment we'd first met Khloe, we'd all been falling in love with her. It manifested itself as lust first, but how else could we all be so wrecked? Why else would I be losing sleep, downing myself in work, and even being noticeably sadder by my colleagues? I was in love. We all were.

Now not only had we lost Khloe, but we were losing Luke too? Shouldn't we be sticking together?

"You can't go," I told Luke.

"I have to," he responded. He stood up from his

chair before I could say anything else. "I can't stay here." He pulled a piece of paper from his pocket and handed it to me. "My flight info. Tell the rest of the guys I'm sorry."

He turned away from me and left without another word. I looked at the paper and my heart sank. He really was leaving the next day at noon. Luke was what held our group together, if he left, it was probably only a matter of time before we were all back off to our solitary lives again. I didn't want him to go, and I knew that the only way Luke would stay is if we could get Khloe back. Maybe it was a shot in the dark. Maybe we'd already lost Khloe, and Luke would go to Miami and that would be it, but I couldn't just sit back and watch everything fall apart.

I picked up my phone and called the same doctor who had covered for me while I was gone for the wedding, Dr. Jillian Portland.

"Cody," she answered. "How are you?"

"I've had better days, Jill," I responded. "I'm pretty sick. Doctors being sick, you never see it coming."

"Too true," she replied. "Are you on tonight?"

"I am, but I'm hoping you might be able to cover for me?" I said.

"I've been looking to get away for the weekend with my husband," she responded slickly.

"You help me out today, and I'll make sure you get a full four days," I said.

Jillian chuckled. "I'm on my way."

I didn't quite know how I was going to convince Khloe to come home, but I had to get the rest of the guys together, and we had to figure it out.

24

CHRISTIAN

I was still in my workout clothes when Cody called to say that we had to have an emergency meeting. Last I heard, he was working all night, so it was bizarre to me to have him call out of the blue and ask everyone to meet at his penthouse. I couldn't imagine what could happen so suddenly that he would need to see everyone right away, but Cody wasn't a dramatic guy, so when he called and said it was an emergency, I believed him. I got to his house as quickly as I could, and I could see that everyone else had moved with the same urgency. Everyone else's cars were already parked on the street outside, apart from Luke's which was missing.

"Typical," I hissed as I noticed his car was the only one missing from the pack. He was behaving as if he was the only one who was torn up about Khloe and didn't even have the respect to show up to an emergency meeting on time.

I made it into Cody's penthouse and saw that all of the other guys were already seated and waiting patiently. Mason, Brett, and David were in similar garb to me; it seemed like they had come directly from training as well, and Bram was wearing a suit as if he had come directly from work.

"Hey," Brett greeted.

"Hi," I said, not seeing Cody anywhere in the living room. "Where's Cody?"

"He hasn't made it back yet. He was just waiting for his cover to make it to the hospital," Bram explained.

So he was working. I knew I'd heard correctly. I sat down on one of the couches and grabbed a beer and waited with the rest of the guys in silence. It made me uncomfortable how disjointed we felt. I thought about how Luke would normally break the ice with some stupid joke, or if Khloe was around, he'd be teasing her and we'd all be enjoying the show. Whether I was mad at him or not, I couldn't deny that he was usually what connected us when we were hanging out, otherwise we were just a bunch of football players in different positions sitting around with a doctor and an accountant. That sort of thing didn't typically happen. It was only because of Luke that any of us would find any common ground.

Finally, the front door opened and closed and

Cody appeared in the living room. He was still dressed in his scrubs from work, and looked as if he'd run a mile in a minute. His hair was frazzled, eyes were wild, and even the pets of his shirt were slightly darker from sweat.

"What the hell happened to you?" Brett asked.

"I didn't drive to work today, I walked, so I had to run home," Cody explained.

"You could have walked," Mason said.

"Or taken an Uber," I added.

"No, we don't have time for that," Cody said. "Luke's leaving."

"What does that mean?" David asked. "From here? He isn't here now."

"No," Cody said. "He's leaving the state, for good. He told me he's up for free agency."

"He wouldn't leave the Hellraisers," Brett said. "Coach already has us prepping for next season. He thinks he's staying."

"He just told me to my face that Miami wants to pick him up and he's going down there tomorrow to hear them out," Cody said. "He's really struggling losing Khloe, and he's taking it all out on himself." He glared at me and then at Brett. "It isn't as if you two helped the situation."

Brett threw his arms in the air. "He is the one who messed up."

"We all messed up," Bram said. "We never should have made that scorecard."

I crossed my arms. "We've made a thousand

scorecards before. We knew things were different once Khloe agreed, why would he—?"

Cody cut me off. "Enough! We can't keep blaming him alone for a mistake we all made. We're all arrogant assholes, and if it had been any of us, we would have done the exact same thing. None of that matters anymore. What matters is that if we want Luke to stay, we need Khloe, and if we want Khloe to come back, we need Luke."

"Oh, that makes a whole lot of sense with one of them in California and the other one headed to Florida," David said.

"We can get Khloe to come back if she realizes that Luke is so sorry that he's going to bail on Texas altogether, and if we can convince Khloe to come back, Luke will stay," Cody said. He looked around at all of us and noticed our skepticism. "What? You guys don't want to be with Khloe?"

We all shifted in our spots. It couldn't be clearer in the room; we all wanted to be with her more than anything. It changed all of our moods in a minute. If it could work to get Khloe back and get Luke to stay, then it was worth it.

"When does his flight leave?" I asked.

"Tomorrow at noon," Cody said, unfolding a paper and passing it around the group. "We have from now until then to get Khloe back in the state of Texas."

"How do we even get Khloe to talk to us?" Bram asked.

"Well, she's the most upset with Luke, right?" Mason said. "So we just have to convince her to forgive him."

We all looked at Mason, generally impressed. He wasn't the 'brains' of our group by any means, and even though he had a degree in Political Science, his intelligence could be categorized as 'street smarts' at best. When it came to practical life application, he wasn't the best guy for the job. However, what he said made sense. Cody was absolutely right, Khloe and Luke were one another's incentive to remain in Texas, and a part of our relationship, so if we could convince Khloe to forgive Luke and come back home, then we could convince Luke not to leave. It was easier said than done, though, Khloe couldn't stand us, and Luke felt too pitiful about himself to play any role in convincing Khloe he was truly sorry.

David stood up, looking irritated. "What are we all staring at our feet for? Luke's our best friend, no one knows us better than him. We've already called Khloe, we've sent her texts, we've sent her emails, so let's go for the only thing we have left, a video. If she can actually see our faces, maybe she'll listen."

Cody let out a sigh. "It's worth a shot." He pulled out his phone and pointed at the glass door leading out to the balcony. "Out there, with the sunset."

We all filed out to the balcony and lined up in a row. Cody started his phone with it flipped towards him to start. "Hey there, stunner. I know you're pissed at us, and we've all said our sorries, but we can admit that this all leads back to Luke. So we have a few things to say about him…"

He flipped the camera towards us and nodded. Bram stepped forward with a shy smile. "Yeah, Luke's an ass, but we don't need to tell you that. What I'd much rather tell you is that he's also the most caring guy I know. When I broke my leg last year, he came and stayed at my place with me for six weeks. He would barely let me piss alone. When he loves, he loves hard, and I know he loves you. He messed up, but I'm hoping you can find it in your heart to forgive him."

David stepped up next. "I wouldn't be on the starting lineup if it wasn't for him. He's got the most integrity of anyone that I know. When he saw that a few of the guys were roughing me up and trying to keep me from displaying my skills, he was willing to risk his career to show Coach that I was worth my salt. I wouldn't be where I am if Luke wasn't the great guy that he is. Dick or not, I can't deny that he's been an amazing friend."

"Luke's pretty cool," Mason said, and then stopped.

"That's it?" Cody said from behind the camera.

Mason shrugged. "What? I'm not gonna sit here stroking his ego."

"He's not gonna see it, it's for Khloe," Cody responded.

Mason let out a loud, exasperated sigh. "I mean,

what? He's a really cool guy! Whenever we go out, people gravitate towards us. Not just women, but guys too. People just wanna be around him." He sighed again. "Honestly, I haven't seen him at all this week and my life just feels…" He let out a gruff and then walked away from the group and back inside the apartment. In a way, it was the most perfect 'Mason' way to show his true feelings.

I looked at Brett and he was looking back at me. It was down to us, the ones who'd taken the greatest issue with Luke. Brett stepped up and I was relieved for a few more seconds to figure my stuff out.

"I'm still pissed at Luke. I'm probably going to be for a while, but not because he fucked this up for us, but because he's had like 10 years to be with you and he wasn't." A bunch of the guys hummed affirmations; we all felt that. "We just met you six months ago, but he's known you since high school. He should have been with you way before now. He's a fucking idiot."

I stepped up. "Yeah, but…" I got it. Luke passed up a great opportunity 10 years ago, but I couldn't bring myself to feel the same way about it that Brett did. "Luke brought us together. Can you imagine if he'd been with Khloe back then? He probably wouldn't have had us start sharing women, hell, he might not even have met us." I looked right at the camera. "Either way you shake it out, we can't deny it. If it weren't for Luke, we wouldn't have ever even met Khloe, we definitely wouldn't have had the bravery to be with her."

Brett smiled and nodded as he realized what I'd said was true. "Regardless of what that dumbass has done to hurt us and you, the fact remains, that he's what brought us together. We have him to thank for what we have, Khloe. We have him to thank for you."

I exchanged looks with Brett again, and it happened for us both at that moment. We forgave Luke, and we definitely didn't want him going to Miami.

We stepped back into the line and Cody turned the camera to face himself again. "We miss you, Khloe. We hate that we lost you, but now we're risking losing Luke too. He's leaving for Miami tomorrow and he may not come back. You're the only thing that would convince him to stay, so now we need you to be the glue that he was before. We promise to spend every day of the rest of our lives apologizing for what we did to hurt you, please. Just come home." Cody stopped recording and then fell silent as he clicked around on his phone. A few moments later he looked up at us, his expression as nervous as we felt. "It's sent."

"What do we do now?" David asked.

"The only thing we can do," I said. "We wait."

25

KHLOE

My heart felt full to bursting. When I saw the video come through on my phone, and heard Cody saying that they had some things to say about Luke, I assumed they were going to bash him in an attempt to get me back. I couldn't have even begun to expect that they were actually going to praise him. They weren't even defending themselves anymore, they were just trying to get me to forgive *him*. I knew they were close, but I had no idea how huge it was. The stories they'd told of Luke caring for them and being an amazing guy shocked me. I was beginning to see it myself back in Puerto Rico, but I didn't anticipate the size. Luke had affected all of these mens' lives in such a profound way, and he had done the same for me.

"Wow," Cece said. She was sitting next to me on the couch and had watched the video over my shoulder. "That was amazing. They really stood up for him. Is this Luke guy really like that?"

All I had thought about for the past week, and really for the past 10 years, was how much of an ass Luke was, but thinking back on it, I'd seen part of his wonderful side too. I watched him take his job as best man to Kent very seriously, I'd seen the way he cared for all of the guys when we were over in Puerto Rico, and I even overheard him telling Cody how he really felt about me when we were on the plane on the way over.

"Yeah," I said. "He's pretty great. I mean, he can be a dick."

"What man isn't?" Cece replied and I laughed. "If he's that great, and obviously all those guys are great, why wouldn't you go back to them?"

"Do I *have* to retell you the scorecard story?" I said.

"No, I heard it, but guess what? Men do stupid shit. They think with the heads below their waists before they think with the ones above it. They all admitted that none of them actually kept track of the points, it was only Luke, and he probably did it to boost his own ego. Guys do dumb stuff when they want to feel better about themselves. And with you walking around, it's hard to feel like the top dog. You're hot stuff." I laughed. I knew that the guys would agree. "Besides, are you really comfortable with being the reason their friendship falls apart? He's clearly what holds them together, and if you don't go home, he's gonna leave and they'll completely unwind."

I hadn't thought about it that way. I didn't want to be the reason that they stopped being friends, and even if it was their actions that led to their downfall, I could get over the scorecard, but they would never recover from Luke leaving for Miami. If the scorecard didn't exist, they may not have ever even made a move.

"So, what are you gonna do?" Cece asked.

I shook my head. "I don't know."

I clicked out of the video and saw the single notification still hanging at the corner of my voicemail app. I still hadn't listened to Luke's voicemail. I clicked the app and pressed play on Luke's voicemail and brought my phone to my ear.

It started with a huge sigh and then silence. I could hear Luke breathing, maybe even sniffling, but then he finally took a deep breath and started. "Khloe, listen. I'm not going to apologize for the scorecard anymore. Not because you don't deserve an apology, but because no amount of sorry that I could say could make up for how demeaning and stupid that was. You mean the world to me and all of the guys, and we knew that you were different from the beginning. I forgot it even existed until I fell out and then I filled it out, for what? Did I expect it to make my dick grow?" He let out a little growl. "You know, it was partly your fault too. You're so fucking sexy that we all started dreaming up these fantastical things to do with you. We didn't honestly think we'd get to, but then you came out the gate a complete freak, and it was kind of hot for me to see all the things we'd already done." He grumbled again. "That's no excuse, and I'm not actually blaming you. I'm not even asking you to forgive me, but don't drag the guys into my stupidity. Mason, Brett, Christian, David, Cody, and Bram; those are good guys. They'll take amazing care of you, and I know you'll be happy with them. Don't let me ruin this for them. Go be with them, and I'll step back. That's what they deserve, and so do you." He sniffled. "I love you, Khloe. I just want you to be happy."

Tears started to streak down my face. He'd done the exact same thing the other guys had done. He defended them. They really loved each other, and I loved them too. The line went dead from Luke's voicemail, but I kept the phone pressed to my ear. Part of me was hoping that if I kept it there, I would hear Luke's voice again, saying wonderful things to me, and assuring me that the scorecard meant nothing.

"I'm so loved," I whimpered to Cece.

"Seems like it," she said. "So what the fuck are you doing here?"

I jumped up from the couch, dropping my phone in the process, and bolted into the spare bedroom I'd been staying in. "I gotta go!"

Cece ran in after me. "Wait, call them! Tell them so that they can stop Luke!"

"Right!" I said. I turned around to head back for my phone.

"Wait!" Cece said. "You need to book a flight! Every second you wait, could be another second wasted."

"True!" I said, and turned around again to head back into the bedroom for my computer.

"Oh no!" Cece said. "Call them! They think you hate them."

"Ugh!" I growled, spinning around again and running for my phone.

"No wait!" Cece said.

I threw my hands over Cece's mouth. "Stop! I'm just running in circles. I don't have time for this."

"Sorry," Cece said. "I'm panicking, but I don't know why."

"Can you grab your computer and look up flights while I call Cody?" I asked.

Cece nodded. "Yes! I'm helpful! I can do that."

Cece rushed off for her bedroom and I went out and grabbed my phone. I sat down on the couch and dialed Cody's number. The phone didn't even trill and entire full ring before I heard the line pick up.

"Khloe?" Cody said.

His voice covered me like a warm blanket. I missed them so much more than I realized. "Hey," I greeted. "I got the video."

"And?" Cody said.

"I'm coming home," I replied.

"She's coming home!" Cody yelled and I heard an eruption of cheers around him; he must have still been with all of the guys. "When are you coming home?"

Cece came and sat down next to me and showed me her laptop screen. She had a flight to Austin pulled up, but it wasn't until 9am the next day. "Uh, the flight is at 9."

"No, 9? We need you here tonight to stop Luke," Cody said. "Is it a price thing? We'll pay for the flight. Fly first class if you need to."

I took Cece's computer and scrolled down to the more expensive flights, but it was no dice. A day before flight to a major state like Texas; everything was full. "There's nothing sooner than that," I said. "Can't you guys just call Luke and tell him I'm coming home?"

"We've been trying to get ahold of him, but he isn't responding to any of us," Cody said.

"Well, fuck, keep trying. I'll get there as soon as I can," I said.

"Okay, we'll see you soon," Cody said, a slight bit of giddiness to his voice.

"Yes you will," I said.

"Hey," Cody said. "We love you."

I felt like that scene from the Grinch where his heart got so big that the metal casing broke. I was coming around to believing that was true, but hearing it made all the difference. "I love you too."

"She loves us!" Cody shouted and all the guys cheered again. "Be safe, beautiful."

The time between California and Texas passed like molasses. I woke up in the morning to find a text from Cody saying that they still hadn't gotten ahold of Luke, but according to their coach he was still getting on the flight to Miami. Even if he eventually learned that I was going back to Texas once he was in Florida, if he made a decision he couldn't undo before he figured it out, he would still be gone for good. I checked my watch when we touched down and was relieved to see that we arrived early. I was down to no other choice. In true, 'end of the romance movie' fashion, I was going to have to run through the airport to try and stop Luke in the final hour.

I started to bolt through the airport, with only five minutes until Luke's flight was going to start boarding.

"Just hang on," I huffed out loud. "I'm coming."

26

BRETT

Maybe it would seem like an incredible waste of money to someone else, but Christian and I agreed, since Khloe couldn't get back in time, and we had created the most dissonance with Luke, it was up to us to go to the airport and buy tickets just to try and stop him. Unfortunately, we underestimated Austin traffic getting to the airport, and then how bad morning security would be and weren't getting there in a timely fashion. We were just rushing out of the checkpoint at 11:30am, and Luke's plane was probably already boarding. Khloe's flight was scheduled to get in pretty shortly as well, so we decided it was best to split up.

"I'll go for Luke," Christian said. "You go get Khloe."

"Call me if you find Luke," I said, and then I rushed off.

People were staring at me through confused expressions as I bolted through the airport, but I didn't care. I had to get to Khloe, and we had to get her to Luke before he got on his plane. I rushed to the gate where Khloe's flight was coming in, and was shocked to see her rushing right at me.

She stopped in her tracks and then continued at me. She collided into me with a kiss, but then pulled away and started off towards Luke's gate. "Hurry your cute ass up!"

I didn't have any time to process what had just happened. Khloe was back, and she just kissed me, but she was already off through the airport. I wanted to stop and take a moment to breathe in a sigh of relief that she confirmed she had forgiven us, but it wasn't the time to focus on that. I turned around, and headed off in the same direction as Khloe. I hadn't gotten a call from Christian, and a glance at a clock as we ran proved that it was officially noon. If he hadn't gotten to Luke in time, he was already on a plane on the way to Miami.

"Hurry up!" Khloe barked. "You're a football player! Get the lead out."

She was hard to keep up with. For a thick girl, who classed herself as not being athletic, and compared to me who was a football player, she was leaving me in the dust. I did want to find Luke, but I wasn't willing to risk injury to do it. I'd just hop a plane and head for Miami and chase him through the airport there. People were all over the place and it felt like they all had rolling bags or kids on leashes; getting through the terminal was like taking on a very difficult obstacle course.

We cleared a crowd of people and time seemed to move in slow motion for a moment. We looked up and saw the gate agent closing the door to the Miami flight. Neither Christian nor Luke was anywhere in sight, and both Khloe and I came to a halt.

"We're too late," Khloe said sadly.

I walked up to her and placed my hand on her back. "Don't worry, we'll figure out a way to get to him before it's too late."

"Before it's too late to do what?" Khloe and I both whipped our heads around and Luke was standing behind us with Christian at his side.

Christian walked up to me and backhanded me across the head. "Ow!" I yelped. "What the fuck was that for?"

"Why is your phone off?" he growled.

I pulled my phone out of my pocket and saw that it was in fact turned off. I must have done it accidentally when I was running through the airport. "Oops," I said.

"You came back," Luke said with a smile. Khloe nodded, but then her eyes rolled back in her head and she started to drop from her feet. "Khloe!" Luke got his hands out just in time to catch her as she passed out into his arms.

He carried her to the nearest set of benches and

helped her sit down. Once she was sitting on the bench, to all of our relief, her eyes started to open. Christian knelt down in front of her and kissed her knees gently. "Are you okay?"

"Yeah, I didn't realize I was that fatigued," she said. "I haven't eaten or drank anything since before you guys sent me your video last night."

"What video?" Luke said.

"I'll get her some water." Christian stood up and disappeared into the crowd, while I took my boarding pass and started to fan Khloe's face.

"What video?" Luke repeated.

"Don't worry about it 135," Khloe spat and both of our jaws dropped. She glared at Luke for a minute and then burst out into laughter. "You should see your faces."

"Not funny," Luke hissed.

"Oh, lighten up…" I chuckled. "…135."

Luke pointed his finger in my face. "I was barely accepting of it when *she* said it, but I'll kick your ass."

Christian came back and handed Khloe a bottle of water and she took a big gulp. When she was done, she started to get to her feet, and we all huddled around her like a toddler just learning how to walk. She pushed us away and then began walking towards the exit. When she was about ten feet away, she looked back over her shoulder and flashed us a huge, brilliant smile.

"Well? Let's go home," Khloe said.

We didn't hesitate. Luke rushed up and took her hand into his and we all walked out of the airport and took our first steps into our new life together.

*W*hat I had learned in the near five months since we started dating Khloe was that whatever she asked for, she received in spades. We balanced our relationship well; we each got our individual time with her. Whenever any of us wanted to 'team up' for sexy time, we managed to make that work as well, but whenever Khloe made a request of any kind, we turned into behemoths each trying to one up one another getting it for her. It was just before the 4th of July weekend, and Khloe mentioned that she wished that she could get away for the holiday, so we planned a barbecue, argued over whose house it was going to be at, who was going to get to cook for her, who was going to get to bake for her, everything from A to Z. We had to play several games of Cody's convoluted football tournament from back when we were in Puerto Rico, but in the end, I got to be the host and everyone else filled in with food and treats. The added bonus was that my house had a nice, big pool, so we got to look at Khloe in a bikini.

"Mason, I swear to god." I was standing at the grill when Khloe's voice shattered my thoughts. I looked over just in time to see Mason grab Khloe and jump into the pool. David and Christian, who were already in the pool, rushed over and immediately started trying to get her top undone. Khloe started to laugh. "Knock it off! Kent and Anna will be here soon!"

I laughed, nearly spitting out the beer I had just taken a sip of, and I felt the fizziness and dusky smell of the hopps singe my nose as I snorted.

"Guys, seriously. Khloe and Kent finally convinced Anna to hang out with us, and we don't want to ruin it by flashing her the second she gets here," Cody explained. He was on a beach chair off to the side with a hefty medical book situated on his knees.

"Luke!" I looked in the other direction and Bram and Brett were getting one of my fold out tables set up. "Here?"

They had the table situated right under the big oak tree that sat in my backyard. "Yeah, that's good. The shade will keep us from getting too hot."

I turned back around and Khloe was climbing out of the pool. For a moment, her eyes met mine and my face warmed. It was crazy how months later she still gave me butterflies in my stomach. I was one lucky guy. She slicked back her hair, wrung out the edges of her bathing suit and then walked over and sat down at the picnic table. Brett and Bram instantly stopped what they were doing to kiss and pet her; it actually made me a little jealous. I returned to the grill and noticed that the food was nearing completion, so I started to pull them off.

"Food's done!" I shouted out.

Everyone gathered just in time for Kent and Anna to arrive, and then we all sat down at the table.

"Hey, you know what I was thinking?" Anna asked as she sat down. "Whatever happened with your friend Jordan?"

She smiled. "She made up with her guys and went back to Dallas." She elbowed Christian as he appeared behind her with a pitcher in his hand. "Not that I have much time to be at my once-again-empty-home now that I have these clowns."

"Who you calling a clown?" Christian started to pour everyone glasses of the spiked lemonades he made from scratch, but when he got to Khloe, she held up a hand to refuse.

"Oh come on, it's your favorite. I made it just for you," Christian said.

"Thank you, but I actually have an announce-ment to make," she said. She looked at me and her face was nearly glowing. She looked back at everyone else and then shrugged her shoulders. "I'm pregnant."

Everyone froze in place. It was completely silent in the yard until Anna stood up and let out a loud, shrill shriek. "I'm gonna be an aunt!"

"And I'm gonna be a father!" David said, then he started fake sniffling.

"Who says you're the dad?" Brett said. "I think it's me."

"Not the way you two do it," Cody said with an eyebrow raised.

Brett settled back into his seat. "Touche."

"It's probably Luke," Mason said.

"Don't boost his ego. I think it's mine," Bram said. "Oh! I have an idea."

Khloe grabbed a nearby knife and held it out towards Bram. "If you even use the word scorecard, I will cut out your vocal cords."

Bram backed up with wide eyes. "I was just kidding." Everyone laughed as Khloe put down the knife.

"Well, not a moment too late for you to get that new, high-profile job, right?" Christian asked.

"Definitely," David winked, "because we already spoil her, we definitely won't pay for literally every-thing the kid needs."

Khloe giggled. "I don't anticipate we'll struggle, but I am excited about this new job. The Fox brothers own one of the most prestigious event planner companies on Earth, and I'm so excited about this interview with them. Who knows? Maybe they'll even let me plan their Dad's wedding." Her eyes widened. "They are two of eight brothers. Eight! Can you imagine? And apparently they're all very active in the entertainment industry. I mean, their dad is THE man who owns this empire, so I'm not even surprised. "

"Eight?" Mason said, then he raised his eyebrows at Khloe. "We've got some catching up to do."

"Yeah, if you're having seven of them," Khloe commented with wide eyes.

We shared another round of laughter and then we got into eating our food. Khloe leaned her head against my shoulder and I kissed her on the fore-head. While everyone was consumed in conversa-tion, I set my lips near her ear.

"I'm not sure who the father is, but as far as I'm concerned, that kid is my own."

Khloe's hand, which was resting on my leg, squeezed gently. "Thank you," she responded.

"No," I said looking across our weird, but happy family. "Thank you."

THE END

Dear reader, thank you so much for taking the chance to read *Seven Groomsmen from Hell* - Book 6 in my new Reverse Harem Romance series: **Love by Numbers**.

The series is getting more and more interesting, isn't it? Did you like our curvy heroine in this story? While the seven men may have made a mistake by making this a game, eventually they made Khloe understand that what they had for her was REAL!

I do hope that you enjoyed the tropical beach vibes of Puerto Rico in this story. I'm starting to get sick of the cold weather, so let's just use our imagination for now, so we can lie on the imaginary beach and watch the waves. :)

And who's excited to read the next one in the series? I bet you are! Because the next one will be even sexier and more panty-melting. There will be

8 delicious Fox brothers, all hot for a lucky lady. That's all I can say for now ;)

Please do **follow me on Amazon** right now, so you never miss my new release again.

And if you haven't read the previous stories, I strongly recommend that you start with the first book: *Two Billionaires' in Vegas.*

ALSO BY NICOLE CASEY

All my books are either FREE or available in Kindle Unlimited!

Love by Numbers
2 Billionaires in Vegas
3 Bosses' Assistant
4 Ranchers' Bride
5 Mafia Captors' Virgin
6 Single Dads' Nanny
7 Groomsmen from Hell

Temptation Next Door Series (COMPLETED)
Hot Dad Next Door
Doctor Next Door
Mr. Fixit Next Door
Author Next Door
Prince Next Door
Firefighters Next Door

Beauty & The Captor Series (COMPLETED)
Her Beast: A Dark Romance
Her Savior: A Dark Romance
Her Dom: A Dark Romance

The Viera Triplets (COMPLETED)
Dirty Pleasures: A Dad's Best Friend Romance
Come Closer: A Romantic Suspense
Six Years Later: A Second Chance Romance

Baby Fever Series (COMPLETED)
Leaving to Stay: A Rock Star Bad Boy Romance
Accidental Soulmates: A Vegas Accidental Marriage
Romance
Can't Get Over You: An Enemies-To-Lovers
Romance
Marrying The Wrong Twin: A Billionaire Marriage
Mistake Romance
Deep in the Mountains: A Mountain Man Romance

Standalone
A Weekend with the Mountain Man
Snow and the Seven Men

Romance Collection
Love, Again
Mercury Billionaires
Sinful Like Us
Beauty & The Captors

ABOUT THE AUTHOR

Nicole Casey is a Contemporary Romance Author born and based in The City of Angels. She writes steamy contemporary romance with a happily ever after.

When she isn't penning sultry scenes, Nicole Casey loves getting lost in her daydreams, going for long nighttime walks, and fine dining. She is also a red wine aficionada and bookworm. Above all, she enjoys nothing more than spending quality time with her loved ones in both human and cat form.

Subscribe to Nicole Casey's newsletter to get her steamy romance story and be the first to hear about new releases: https://dl.bookfunnel.com/lzcjb30i6u

Follow Nicole on BookBub to learn more about her books: https://www.bookbub.com/profile/nicole-casey